OVATION BY DEATH

Also by Dorian Yeager

Cancellation by Death
Eviction by Death
Murder Will Out

OVATION BY DEATH

Dorian Yeager

A Vic Bowering Mystery

St. Martin's Press
New York

OVATION BY DEATH. Copyright © 1996 by Dorian Yeager. All rights reserved. Printed in the United States of America. No part of this book may be used or reproduced in any manner whatsoever without written permission except in the case of brief quotations embodied in critical articles or reviews. For information, address St. Martin's Press, 175 Fifth Avenue, New York, N.Y. 10010.

Library of Congress Cataloging-in-Publication Data

Yeager, Dorian.
    Ovation by death / by Dorian Yeager. —1st ed.
      p.   cm.
    ISBN 0-312-14022-3
    1. Women detectives—Maine—Fiction. 2. Actresses—Maine—Fiction. 3. Maine—Fiction. I. Title.
PS3575.E363O9   1996
813'.54—dc20   95-30033

First edition: April 1996

10 9 8 7 6 5 4 3 2 1

ACKNOWLEDGMENTS

*Steve and my Miss Elle's surrogate family;
the growing cast of friendly spirits, directed by the
immortal Fran Stevens;
those who love me and those who suffer me;
the City of Prague for giving my
evil twin and me back our vacationing Muse;
and, always, the dream team:
Reagan Arthur and Fran Lebowitz*

For my sister, Pat:
the first imaginary corpse in my closet,
the sane one when I am crazy and
the crazy one when I am crazed
with sanity

PROLOGUE

IT WAS EAST Port Noplace, Maine, on a relatively balmy night. Since it was blackfly season, the double barn doors were closed and several overlarge electric fans wheezed in direct opposition to the rhythm of flailing feet. The intricate musical number involving the entire cast was less a whiz-bang showstopper, more a free-for-all St. Vitus' dance. The manual spotlight blew up the first time it was turned on, leaving the more lyrical, sensitive moments lit up like the local Kmart during a blue-light special.

In other words, the opening night performance was uneventful.

The scrim curtain got jammed twice and a scene change took so long that the audience thought it was the intermission and left to get drinks and stretch their legs. Other than that—and aside from the fact that *I* hadn't been cast in the lead role of Miss Mona, madam of *The Best Little Whorehouse in Texas*—the evening of entertainment had been a good one.

At least by summer stock standards, which tend to be more negotiable than, say, Broadway.

The audience believed they had gotten their twelve dollars' worth, the cast firmly believed they had been brilliant, and the producers were profoundly relieved and more than a little grateful to have "gotten through another one."

It ended less well for the Miss Mona who wasn't—bless the poor taste and judgment of the casting director—me.

At the opening night party held at the cast house next door to the theater, the chorus missed the leading lady (as much as is possible for people getting paid less to do more) and sent the person with the fewest credentials and most years to endure toward legal drinking age to find her.

The overworked and underimbibed intern who pulled this noxious assignment located Miss Mona easily enough in her nonsmoking dressing room.

The leading lady was inelegantly welded to a shorted-out blow dryer. And, may I point out, smoking to beat the band despite the two-foot-square sign of prohibition tacked to the door.

Interns always get the crap jobs. It's called paying dues, or passing the buck. You choose. I chose to skip that whole intern (working twenty-seven hours a day for bad food and experience) part. It was one of the few decisions I have made that were ever 100 percent sound; but, we'll get around to my love life later.

The Hempstead Beach police arrived quickly, albeit far too late for the leading lady, and kept the surviving cast members awake and sober longer than had Miss Mona foregone her post-show primping ritual and just gotten down to hard drinking.

Given the perfectly natural shock and ensuing chaos, I was

not called to get my quick-study butt on a plane to replace the late diva until 5:00 A.M.

That was the musical director's fault, but I didn't blame him for yanking me out of my beauty sleep when I found out he was calling to hire me for two shows and four weeks toward a new unemployment claim.

To coax me into an utterly impossible job, he reminded me we'd done the show twice before—together and I'd done it twice more on my own, though probably not as well. (His opinion, not necessarily mine—though he was right.)

Given the off-putting dead star situation and the fact that I'd be thrown unprotected and unprepared into the role that same day, he offered me about three times my going rate. Lucky for him, I come cheap, if not easy. Then he dangled the real bait: the second show.

Not only had I spent the debatably best years of my life repeating the same roles and figured it was damned near time to "stretch," the second show was a brand-spanking new musical he'd written all by his little self that had a really, really, really good chance (*everyone* said so) of being brought into New York on (at the very *least*) an Off-Broadway contract. *Everyone* said so.

He didn't need to mention any of that extraneous, unfounded delusional stuff. I'm an actor.

The only illusions I have left are those I create in front of an audience for a paycheck. Being a thirty-ninish struggling actor, I also realize that means I don't have a (pardon my use of the "F" word) future beyond a present contract.

It is because of such a low standard of expectation that we theater folk subsist on platitudes.

"All I need is a big break." "The play's the thing."

"There's no business like show business." "Th-th-th—that's all, folks!" Ha. But, not me, baby.

Anyway, I was broke, and "the show *must* go on."

Wouldn't I love to get ahold of the first moron who said *that*.

ONE

"You don't respect me," Sergeant Dan Duchinski pronounced upright from the great sag his backside had punched at the edge of my mattress. I threw an extra pair of black dance pants on the tangle of formless spandex arms and legs piled in the suitcase at the foot of my platform/drawer bed.

"That's stupid," I argued intelligently on my hands and knees, voice muffled by the clothing in the closet, where my face was buried. I was searching for at least one pair of shoes that matched. "Everyone knows I think you're the best cop in New York City. Aha!" I added, optimistically believing I had two shoes that went together as a pair. "I respect you like motherhood and the American way."

"No, you don't." Dan picked up and stroked his backup male perspective, Slasher, my rescued alley cat. He put on his most seriously jaded law enforcement face and flipped Slasher on his back to ruffle his stomach. "It's because I'm a man, isn't it?"

"That's stupid," I answered again, too busy to be clever for a change, not to mention to admit to a basic bias and probable character flaw. Revealed in the overhead light I could see that the two ballet slippers I held in my hands were separated by several years of wear, tossed the older of the two over my shoulder, and plunged back into the clogged drain I like to call my wardrobe. "I've done everything but present myself naked on the bed with an apple in my mouth to get you to have sex with me." I pulled out a pair of character shoes, sans taps. They were red, but what the hell. "Excuse me, but most men would find that damned respectful."

"I rest my case," Dan said. He cradled the cat in his burly arms and let the elderly animal chew on his big hand. "Notice you said 'have sex' and not 'make love.' We're adults, not hyperthyroidal adolescents." Easy for him to say. I, myself, was peaking, rapidly.

"Oh, God," I moaned, wondering for the thousandth time how I could get myself involved with a man who found my legally married-but-separated categorical distinction enough to preclude some mutually satisfying physical encounter.

Or really hot, squooshy sex. Whatever.

"What?"

I pulled myself out of the wall of mashed clothes. "I said, 'Oh, God,'" I repeated. You have to understand that I love this man enough to put up with a lot of Chinese food and very little noogie noogie. Three years' worth. That is quite a bit. I wanted to be empathetic. I wanted to comfort him. I wanted to finish packing. "My sweet honey-drawers, I know what this is really all about." I sagged next to Dan on the bed, resigned to spending time I didn't have being Mother Earth understanding. I hate being nuturing, but it is the way I was drug up. Thanks, Mom.

"No, you don't," he rejected me. Yes, he knew I did, but he was going to deny it—being a man and all.

"Yes, I do." I leaned against his muscular shoulder. And arm. And thigh. And tried to be rational. "This is your my-woman-is-going-on-the-road-and-will-undoubtedly-be-boffing-her-leading-man thing."

"Give me a little credit, Vic." He tried to bump me away from his side. "I am not a child." His lower lip stuck out petulantly. It was very cute, given the size and pugnaciousness of the face.

"Of course not." I tried to remember whether or not I had put my favorite rehearsal shoes in my parents' basement the last time I was home during one of my "getting-out-of-the-business" phases. "It's just that you really do care about me, even if you won't, uh, make love to me. Your reaction is perfectly normal and natural." (Stupid, but mundane, though I didn't say *that*). "I've been through it before with what's-his-ex-name."

That would be my almost-ex-husband, Barry, who wouldn't turn down a little slap-and-tickle with Bella Abzug on the median strip of the Massachusetts Turnpike.

Believe it or not, I was trying to be honest, yet kind. It's just that I was catching a plane in three hours and didn't have a lot of time to spend on diplomatic niceties.

"Barry's not your ex. You're not divorced yet," Dan grumped. Slasher snored in total male agreement.

I wasn't about to get into that dialogue again. Through past performances, I knew the play to run several days—sort of the *Nicholas Nickleby* of relationship discussions. I gave up and threw the mismatched pair of shoes into the Pullman and zipped it up.

"Thanks for babysitting the apartment and Slasher," I said, and in a last-ditch conciliatory effort ran my hand up the inside of Dan's thigh from my position on the floor.

He fluffed my already tousled explosion of red hair. Taking

this to be encouragement, I rose to my knees and presented my face for kissing.

My hopes were high: packing to go on the road has been known to elicit some very hot, spontaneous reactions in the loved ones we leave behind to feed the cat and pick up the mail.

Dan obliged with a slow, melancholy smooch. His heart did not seem to be in it, but it was an intro.

No fool, I slithered up between his legs and lay over his now prone body, blazing a trail of fluttery kisses up his neck and along his jawline. Also no fool, Dan flipped me to my side and ran his left hand down my side, pulling me to him.

"I'm going to miss you," I whispered smokily into his ear, my fingers tangled in the hair at the nape of his neck. Actually, I knew I would be too busy to miss much of anything for the whole time, but there was no need for him to know that. He pulled back slightly, eyes narrowed, to gaze intimately at me.

And sat up.

"Do you have your script?" he asked.

What?

"What?"

"Do you have your script? You have to go on tonight," he reminded me, and walked away into the living room with the overstuffed suitcase.

Typical. At least he was perceptibly bent over due to some hormonal discomfort. I am woman enough to admit, I hoped portions of his body were absolutely NYPD blue.

Frustrated as always by my seductive incompetence with Dan, I followed him. Okay, I may have whined a little even though I pride myself on never doing that.

"Dan, we have three hours."

He plunked himself on the sofa. Slasher plunked himself on Dan.

"Half hour preflight. One and a half hours' safe travel time to LaGuardia. You haven't changed the message on your answering machine, learned your lines, or shown me where Slasher's food is kept."

"I've done the show four times, and the cat food is in the cabinet where you always stash your piece." I was entering snit territory and using cop slang. Dan hates that.

"It's a gun," he said. "Change your message, and I'll run you through your lines."

Now, I've always been something of a perfectionist on stage. I don't rewrite the playwright or goof around when I'm getting paid to act. Still, having only fifteen hours' notice before being expected to strut my stuff in front of an audience is a strange relief from my usual anal-retentiveness.

Logic dictates: it is not possible to have a perfect show under such circumstances, so how could anyone blame me for screwing up? And if logic says so, I'll believe it. Unfortunately, Dan also had a point.

I hadn't done the show in more than two years and couldn't remember a single line. Even *I* realized that this could cause difficulties for my fellow cast members if—rather than respond to their words with Miss Mona words—I simply stared at them like a cow watching a slowly passing train.

So I changed my message, giving the number of the theater—on the wild off-chance that my agent might call—and let Dan hold book while I quickly realized that the entire libretto and score of *The Best Little Whorehouse in Texas* had miraculously been swallowed into the pulsating black hole of my long-term memory.

"*Zabar's!*" My short-term memory was still intact.

As a new cast member, I was obligated to spend my first week's salary on lox, bagels, and cream cheese from the most legendary of New York delis. Fortunately, it was less than a block away from my apartment.

"No," Dan smacked my knee with the ragged script.

"If you run interference, I can be in and out in ten minutes," I reasoned.

"I'm not that tough," Dan protested, referring to the mind-boggling aggressiveness of Zabar's shoppers, but he followed me out the door. I guess I'd beaten him into submission, and he *had* played defensive linebacker in college. I can be a pretty tough broad myself, especially when I don't give my opposition time to argue.

You see, Zabar's is legendary not only for having the most of everything in the world and at the best prices, but for being crammed to the gorgonzola with the most belligerent, sharp-elbowed little old ladies on the face of the earth.

Not one or two, but every single one of them still hang on to life out of sheer spleen and a fifty-dollar manicure.

I plunked Dan down in the bread line while I slammed myself through the bodies blocking the prepackaged lox and cream cheese. I was asked several times precisely who the fuck I thought I was to which I gave my standard New York City answer: "Taller than you, Stumpy," (sorry, Mom) and dashed back to the bread line. Mistake.

In positioning my elbows at ninety degree angles from my sides to fend off handbasket bruises, I missed the three blue-hairs who squashed their calcium-deprived little old bodies ahead of

Dan so that they could start *thinking* about what sort of bread *might* appeal to them.

When the ancients were finished mulling, there were nothing but plain and onion bagels left, but Dan steadfastly refused to drop by H&H Bagels for sesame, and I decided to be nice.

Okay, so Dan decided I would be nice.

By the time we loaded Dan's little red Toyota and were on our way to the airport, I was pretty darned certain I was going to barf with anxiety.

Dan drove, and I scribbled a cheat sheet into a notepad from my purse. Hand shaking noticeably, I wrote the line that was my cue to speak, my line, and exit cue. Even with a traffic jam on the Triboro Bridge, I barely finished by the time we pulled into the short-term parking lot.

"Why don't you ever listen to me?" Dan asked, hefting my baggage from the trunk.

"It's a matter of principle," I answered, brazen but nonetheless nauseated.

I almost added that I don't tell Dan *his* police business, but it was such a monumental lie I couldn't get it past my dry lips. He knew that and raised his eyebrows in smug confirmation.

"I shouldn't have to mention this," he smugged onward, "but I'm not so thrilled about the way you got this role. I don't want to have to remind you that a woman died under what might be suspicious circumstances."

"Surely this isn't the first blow-dryer electrocution you've ever heard of. This is New York City, for heaven's sake. My last landlord—God rest his soul in the bowels of hell—was fried like calamari by the hot water heater in my very own basement."

"And," he overplayed his smug, "as I remember, that was murder. I would like it if you came back to Slasher undamaged."

"Obviously," I up-smugged him, "you haven't hung around with a lot of dancers. I, personally, will be one big bruise by the middle of next week. Didn't I tell you the story about when I fell off the stage into . . ."

"The lap of a man in a wheelchair who promptly had a heart attack and had to be carried off to the hospital while the show went on, yeah, yeah, yeah. But, wise-ass, you weren't the one who died."

"He didn't die," I objected.

"Yeah, yeah."

His chronic rightness was more annoyingly illustrated by the fact that, had it not been for the flashing of his gold police shield, I wouldn't have made it to the gate before my commuter flight to Portland, Maine, finished loading.

To top it off, I was having the nicotine fit from hell. No smoking in Dan's car, no smoking in LaGuardia Airport, no smoking on the plane; and to further aggravate my nasty craving, I'd been futilely trying to cut down all morning (that was *hours*) in anticipation of musical-comedy vocal stress.

Did I mention my debilitating fear of flying?

I dry-swallowed a tranquilizer and popped a piece of nicotine-laced gum into my Mojave desert of a mouth.

"Okay?" Dan's voice came at me through the white noise of my anxiety attack.

"What?"

"I *said*," Dan repeated, "I'll drive up on Saturday to see the show." He pushed me toward the impatient flight attendant, who was about to hermetically seal me into the dual-prop tuna can of death to Maine. "And good luck."

"*Break a leg!*" I nearly shrieked. "It's 'break a leg,' not *good luck!* That's the worst luck in the world, to wish an actor 'good luck.' "

"Saturday," he responded benignly, handing me over to the steward. "Take another Valium."

The one-hour flight to Portland took one and a half hours due to the fact that we were flying in a motorized kite against the wind, low enough to peek into suburban bedrooms the whole way.

The twelve-year-old boy in the seat behind mine delightedly shouted *"Wind shear!"* every time the impossibly tiny plane was slapped downward—sans my stomach—a few hundred feet toward the growing density of evergreens and granite outcroppings.

I took some solace in the fact that I was sitting in the emergency exit seat, and if we crashed, I would be the first to get out and could probably reset the door so the little towheaded shit would be trapped like a rat in the rubble.

Usually I can repress those kind of antisocial fantasies, but I was feeling a lot of stress.

I thought it was stage fright.

Someday I'm going to be able to figure out the difference between that and "life fright."

TWO

Jonathan Resnick, the musical director and composer, met my plane—which was a very good thing, since the tranquilizer kicked in and slowed me down just about the time the Beechcraft 1900's wheels hit the tarmac.

Regional theater's answer to Leonard Bernstein stood backlit like Mozart's dead father in the doorway to Portland International Jetport, waiting for me to hustle on foot across the hot top from the plane.

Six foot four, two hundred and forty pounds, Stalin mustache, and gayer than laughter, Jonathan had spent two decades frightening the spit out of every man, woman, child, or other he had ever directed. I'd gotten over my intimidation after I caught him remaking one of my costumes for an indigent transvestite just before the Halloween Parade in Greenwich Village.

Jonathan twitched nervously and checked his watch four times by the time I reached him, then turned immediately to the airport and headed in the wrong direction.

"Baggage claim is to the right, Jonathan." I wasn't being

clairvoyant; my sister, Lydia, lives about twenty minutes from the theater and I'd made the flight dozens of times before—back when you could smoke in-flight, not that I begrudge the government with its stupid, self-indulgent, Big Brother rules.

I remembered I hadn't even had time to call and warn my baby sister that I was going to be in the area. Probably just as well. Her husband, for reasons I pretend not to understand, thinks I'm a bad influence on his wife and their impressionable children.

Go figure.

"You didn't check your luggage, did you?" Jonathan asked, as though he had never even considered anything so idiotic in his life.

"I'm good, Jonathan," I answered testily, "but I'm not so good that I can pack for four weeks in a carry-on."

"Right," he said, and grabbed my arm to lead me to the baggage area. "It's already ten o'clock, and an hour to the theater. We don't have much time to walk you through your blocking."

"I have to find a phone, Jon."

"Are you crazy?"

Why do people keep asking me that?

"I want to call my sister, Jon."

"You mean your parents did it *twice?*" He raced ahead. "Sorry. Forget it. There's not a sane person in the world who'd try and do what we're going to try tonight." The testimonial to my instability was somehow reassuring. "This may be nothing more than the pine pitch capital of the nostril of America, but there's still going to be a paying audience who *will* notice if you make a total asshole of yourself. And that," Jonathan picked up his pace, "would make *me* look like an asshole, and then I'd have to kill you myself and recast again. Give your sister a break and let her find out you're here through the cruddy newspaper reviews like everyone else."

It was a more subtle direction than I was used to from Jonathan, but enough to pull me out of my pharmaceutically induced tranquility.

I had committed myself to an impossible job. After costuming, blocking, and rehearsing with the orchestra, I would barely have time to slap on some makeup and find my way out of the wings.

I lit a cigarette in the no-smoking baggage claim area, figuring to get a few really good drags before someone in an alligator shirt and L. L. Bean jackass pants told me to put it out. Fortunately, since mine was the last bag on in New York, it was the first off in Vacationland.

"And," Jonathan added, whipping the heavy suitcase off the baggage carousel with more upper-body strength than I would have credited him with, "it'll take some time to find out how much havoc you've wreaked on your vocal cords with those damned cancer sticks. You and your leading man will probably be singing in the same key."

Jonathan's a big man, and even I of the thirty-five-inch inseam had to scurry to keep up with him as he darted between cars to get to the parking garage and the company van.

We drove out of the airport and past the East Mall, headed north on I-95 toward . . . I realized I didn't even know exactly where the theater was located.

"You still married to what's-his-face?" Jonathan asked, accelerating to approximately the speed of sound.

"Barry," I coached. "No. Well, yes. Sort of."

"Oh, terrific," Jonathan muttered, "I've got a stand-in leading lady with Alzheimer's."

"We're separated," I cut to the chase.

"About time." He cut closer to the front of the chase and changed the subject. He examined me out of the corner of his eye. "All right. So, you didn't get too blowzy while my back was turned; we ought to be able to shoehorn you into the old costumes." So much for sentiment. "I'm using the same blocking from the last time we basted this turkey, so you shouldn't get hopelessly lost on stage.

"The last Miss Mona was almost as much of a cow as you are, so there's no new choreography you wouldn't be able to manage, either."

Now, don't think Jonathan doesn't love and respect me. He does. It's just that there is a certain amount of verbal abuse he finds necessary to keep actors on their toes. We have discussed this, rather loudly and at length, but he's the director and it's a rule that he always wins. Anyway, in his own fashion, he was attempting to reassure me that any no-talent boob in the world could carry off this shot-out-of-a-cannon guest appearance.

"So what's the cast like?" I asked, lighting another cigarette.

"Don't talk," he answered, as he grabbed the cigarette from my fingers and put it in his own mouth. "You're on complete vocal rest and a nonsmoker until I say so. It would be just my luck for you to get nodes on your cords and be struck dumber than usual during your first number."

He tore up to the toll booth, threw money at the woman taking tolls, and tore out again before the go-ahead light engaged. Returning to the subject at hand, he went on.

"In answer to your question, the interns are all still aspiring to attain food chain status," Jonathan continued. "Everyone else is passable except Garrett's—oops, sorry, your—understudy. If she could even *spell* food chain, you'd be back in the city, and I wouldn't be having an ulcer attack." I shot him a look that would kill a less proudly bitchy person, and he kindly backtracked. "I actually asked for you to do the role first, but the leading man came with the late- and not-so-great Garrett Heinrich as a package deal. You're gonna be fine." He frowned. "At least you're breathing."

Fine. Now *there's* a testimonial. Every actor's nightmare of a review: "Victoria Bowering was *fine* in the lead as Miss Mona." Gad.

The rest of the drive was spent with Jonathan trying to break a new land-speed record and me hanging onto the sides of my bucket seat.

You would have been proud of me. I squelched several shrieks of terror because I was more afraid of Jonathan if I broke vocal rest than I was of French kissing a pine tree at ninety miles per hour. I clenched an unlit cigarette between my teeth as though it was a bullet.

The theater was an old whitewash barn with matching outbuildings off a gravel road deep in the coniferous forest.

Up a steep path I could make out a sagging farmhouse, less well-maintained, but no less large. A few shutters were missing, but the residence sported an impressive porch with numerous orphaned chairs and a four-person glider for evening rocking. Crows cawed and cowbirds mimicked the crows. The tiniest chipmunk I had ever seen watched our arrival with sharp eyes from a granite perch on the meandering stone wall and then darted into an imperceptible hole. Obviously, a very smart rodent.

Pine cones crackled beneath the tires, and a fir bough scratched like fingernails across the roof as we parked at a space marked "Don't even think about it." The theater was completely deserted.

"Oh, this is reassuring," I muttered.

"Shut up, Vic," Jonathan warned me and unlocked the small stage door at the side of the barn, behind a stand of mildewed lilacs.

"Charming," I defied him, picking a broken branch out of my hair and following him through the door into the "green room."

I was a bit surprised to note that this waiting area was actually painted green. The air was chilled and wet as befit a summer stock theater during its first production of the season. Later I knew it would become cloying and musky.

"Where's my dressing room?" I asked as my eyes inspected dim corners and cubbyholes. Jonathan hit the light switch without speaking.

Stretched loosely over the door with the bright crimson slash of a NO SMOKING!!! sign lolled two strips of yellow plastic tape.

"I guess I'll take the 'Police Line Do Not Cross' suite," I said and opened my purse. "I am assuming the cops finished here."

"I should have known nothing would keep you out of the star's dressing room."

"Damned right." I opened the door to a six-by-seven-foot cubicle encircled with several mismatched strings of makeup lights and tossed my purse on the wig shelf. There was a damp stain on the floor in front of the small porcelain sink and scorch marks up the wall.

Jonathan noticed my noticing.

"We're going to have an intern touch that up."

"What a *fine* idea," I said, turning my back.

Finished with deep thoughts and ready to get down to the business of show, I XXed out the NO on the smoking sign, and hung a stupid little gold cardboard star beneath it on the door. It was a gift from my long-time mentor, Jewel LaFleur, and irreverent as it may have seemed, I could not have gone onstage—even for rehearsal—without it being there. We actors are a superstitious bunch.

With good reason.

Apparently, we are quite unlucky.

THREE

THE GHOST LAMP (an old superstition that a stage should never ever be left in total darkness) was glowing dully in the center of the deserted planking. Jonathan had disappeared into the hovering shadows to the rear of the audience space by the time I shuffled my way from the green room. Instinctively, I sucked in the dank air to center myself before getting down to the business of becoming a totally different person from the ditzy Victoria Bowering.

There is a hollowness of sound in an empty theater, as though natural human noises are somehow gobbled into a third dimension a foot from where they originate.

"Bowering!" Jonathan's disembodied voice called from what I assumed was the light bridge, above and before me. "Don't move around until I get the work lights on." His instructions fell like a thud at my feet. "Last thing I need is for you to fall off the stage and break your neck. Speaking of which, start stretching out—in place—so we can get to the choreography right away without you tearing something."

Good point. I like to think I am good with pain, but that does not mean I want to invite it over to live with me.

I dropped forward and grabbed my ankles. I meant to grab my toes but fell short, much to my chagrin. Visions of torn Achilles tendons danced through my mind in tempo to the slow bouncing motion futilely intended to get my face nearer and nearer to my knees. The sound of my own breathing grew in direct proportion to my frustration. Age is a frightening thing.

I concentrated and pushed my fingertips closer to the floor. The stained oak stripping became the most important thing in the world to me as I bobbed relentlessly, just like those stupid bill-dipping plastic toy ducks from my childhood: butt in the air, nose in the glass of water.

Kablowww!

A gunshot cut through the heavy air at the same moment the work lights came on and blinded me. I am hardly at all ashamed to admit that I hit the deck. Rather unnecessarily hard, I suppose, but it seemed like the right thing to do at the time.

"Jonathan?" I called to the back of the theater. "Jonathan? Are you all right?" I squinted into the harsh lights, still on my belly. I strained to hear any confirmation from the musical director but the noise gremlins were gobbling faster than my eyes could adjust to the blare of light. "Jonathan." Silence. *"Jonathan!"*

A flame burst two feet from my nose at the lip of the stage. Smoke wafted across my sweaty brow.

"Oh, well," Jonathan intoned from the orchestra pit, "aren't *you* pretty?"

The stage left exterior door opened, framing a medium-sized man in the outside light. The man was carrying a shotgun.

He stepped forward, closing the door behind him and leaving me to once more try to adjust my eyes. I could not control the wry observation that somehow I had become trapped in a Jean-Paul Sartre play—*No Exit,* perhaps—instead of a good, old-fashioned musical comedy.

"Get up, Vic," Jonathan ordered. "We don't have time to sweep the stage right now."

I closed my eyes and heard the metallic clunk of the shotgun as strong hands grasped me from behind and swung me upward and around. And lifted me off the ground. And hugged me. And patted my face. And hugged me again.

"Little Jon?" I asked from beneath a torrent of kisses.

"I couldn't wait to see you!" the shotgun man answered, and swung me around one final time. He was, indeed, Jonathan's lover, Jonathan dubbed Little Jon so that people would not lose their minds trying to sort the two Jonathans out during chaotic rehearsal periods. The name was apt.

Little Jon was around five nine or ten and had the angular athletic build of a dancer. Were he a cross-dresser, he would have fit neatly into my wardrobe.

"I'm the dance captain for the two shows!" he announced with pride.

"Thank God," I breathed. "I was scared to death."

"Don't worry about a thing," Little Jon reassured me about the wrong issue. "We'll cover for you if you get an attack of stupid gas."

"I know that," I said. "I was more worried about an armed and dangerous man shooting me." I kicked at the abandoned shotgun on the stage.

"Oh," Little Jon answered, "I'm also the prop master. I was just checking to make sure the gun worked for your 'mad scene' in the second act."

Panic ripped at my gut. If I were so brain-dead that I could have completely forgotten that my character shoots a damned shotgun round into the air over the heads of the audience, how was I ever going to remember the damned lyrics to the damned "Bus From Amarillo"?

"Is the love fest over?" Big Jonathan asked, hefting himself out of the orchestra pit.

"The gun's been jamming," Little Jon explained.

"Jam this," Jonathan pronounced in his own sweet way and walked to the piano set up at the back of the stage. "Band is on stage, like always, so don't fall into the pit; there won't be drums for you to bounce off this time."

Okay, so *once* I fell into the orchestra pit. *One* time, and you would think I could not find my way across a chorus line. The knot in my stomach tightened. I opened my mouth to object, but Jonathan held up his hand.

"You," he pointed at Little Jon, "go bring in Miss Mona's costumes. Cow-woman here can try them on while I run her through her vocal numbers."

"I hope we don't have to let them out," Little Jon muttered on his way off stage right.

Me, too.

"And you," Jonathan barked at me. "Get yourself somewhere stage center for your opening number."

The sound of the piano immediately hammered through the empty theater. I fumbled to center stage wondering whether or not I had the line that cued the song. It was a big production number with virtually the entire cast involved.

I knew I made my first entrance from the stairs and talked to the two new girls, and that I had some sympathy stuff to say— no, no, the sympathy stuff came before the *second* . . .

"Bowering!" The piano had stopped. "Are you waiting for the second coming, or what?"

"I was just trying to remember how the song gets cued."

"A chord, Bowering," Jonathan played it. "A chord." He hit it. "This one." He hit it again.

"I meant my line."

"We'll worry about lines later," he barked. "Right now I'm worried about the music. This is a *musical,* darling. This is *summer stock.* People don't give a shit about what you have to say."

He struck the opening chord one more time and glowered. I faced the abandoned audience seats and, miraculously, started to sing.

As my voice bounced back at me from the rear of the house, I marveled that I seemed to remember the words and that, despite my self-destructive habits, I could still fill the room with what could be taken as a singing voice. As though possessed, the choreography started to return as well.

I was soaring, moving and interacting with a chorus that I had not yet even met. I twirled and gestured and smiled and arched my eyebrow in that oh-so-Vic-Bowering way. I have, and struck my final pose for the overwhelming audience applause.

All right, I was wheezing a little, but I had gotten from the beginning all the way to the end.

"What was that?" Jonathan asked through clenched teeth.

I knew better than to answer, but did anyway.

"Pissant?" I responded, using the shorthand title to the song.

"No," Jonathan shook his head. "The grand mal seizure you were having."

"I'm not warmed up," I protested.

"You could be boiled in oil for all the good it would do. Never mind." Never *mind?* "Haul ass stage left for the second number." Never *mind?* "You have the cue line, which we will worry about after music." *We?* "Speak."

Little Jon came out of the wings with a pile of feathers and satin, which I recognized to be Miss Mona's wardrobe. "Ruff, ruff, ruff," he laughed. I knew better.

"Shut up," Jonathan ordered. "Bowering, start stripping so I can see what has to be remade for your middle-aged body. You don't move in this number, anyway. Now, speak!"

"Girl," I gave my cue and the piano came up behind me, as did a turquoise blue satin evening gown.

It was a beautifully cut garment that left my entire left arm and shoulder exposed. The right arm was encased in a sleek, long sleeve; the body of the dress smoothed in a long, straight line to the floor, interrupted only by the hip-high slash on the right leg. It was fabulous. I could feel myself becoming Miss Mona at last.

Little Jon unzipped me, muttering, "Good thing we don't have to find a place for a body mike in this thing."

My voice cracked as I stretched to hit the note where my range always broke. In a way it was a comfort. Even though it was an inadequacy, at least it was a familiar one.

As the long afternoon progressed, I got better. Of course, the rehearsal process is surreal by its very nature. There you are, singing and dancing your brains out to an empty room, which always feels incredibly appreciative. I have often thought that I must have quite a fan club spread out over the entire country consisting entirely of bats and field mice.

Unfortunately, rodents are not all that much help when you forget a line or need a sugar daddy.

Which I did all afternoon. As soon as I relearned one segment, I would forget another. Jonathan was as supportive as I have ever known him to be.

"My God," he complained, "it's almost half-hour." Half-hour is the time that the cast has to report and sign in so that the stage manager may be assured that no one has dropped from the face of the earth or eloped with a kazillionaire to Zaire, leaving a big hole onstage where a body should be. Bile crawled up my throat. "There's a shower in the men's dressing room. Take one. You look like shit." I nodded and choked down the buckets of saliva that were dumping into my mouth. Jonathan smacked my cheek. "Costumes look great; I'm going to get something to eat."

And he left me standing there, alone, like a pimple on prom night.

I couldn't move. All I could think was: they can't make me do this. No one can put a gun to my head and say, "Vic, if you don't go out there and humiliate yourself in front of a sold-out audience, we will shoot your cat." I could simply walk out the stage door, hitch a ride to Portland, get on a plane, and forget the whole thing. I could.

It was not against the *law,* after all, to run like a rat deserting a sinking ship. Naturally, I would never get work again. That was only fair. The show must go on. Who said the show must go on? God? Newt Gingrich? Camille Paglia? Who?

"You must be the new Miss Mona."

"What?" I jumped something less than a foot.

"Hi, I'm Mike, your stage manager."

This should have been reassuring. Stage managers are like mothers, only better. They tell you what to do and where to be, they fix things that get broken, hug you when you cry, and do not care whether or not you are a virgin. Unless I had missed my guess, my savior and stage manager *was* a virgin: all gangling limbs and irritated complexion. Mike was eighteen, if he was a day.

Not much of a choice in a stage manager.

"Intern?" I asked hopelessly.

"Uh-huh," Mike nodded ingenuously. "I'm the one who found the body!"

"Uh-huh," I answered and dragged myself to my dressing room.

"Half-hour!" Mike shouted to the cast that had not yet arrived.

FOUR

THERE IS AN actor's nightmare that I never have. It involves being backstage ready to make an entrance when, suddenly, the dreamer realizes that she has never rehearsed the play.

As a fast study, this has happened to me too many times in real life to waste precious REM sleep dealing with other actors' neuroses.

In *my* nightmare, I am backstage getting ready to make an entrance in a play I have never rehearsed, but unfazed because I have a script planted in the wings. I know I can simply memorize one scene, go on and perform it, go offstage and memorize the next scene, ad nauseam. I am calm. I am confident.

And then I realize that I have no idea whatsoever which character I am portraying. As nightmares go, it is pretty Machiavellian. The only variation on this theme is when I dream I do not know what *costume* I am supposed to be wearing and cannot find anything at all that fits me.

Art was imitating life one more time. I was already wearing my opening outfit and I knew which clothes I ended in, but the middle parts were all a blur of pounding adrenaline—approximately the last thing I needed at that moment.

"Vic. Vic, Vic, Vic, she can't *believe* it!"

I did say "approximately" the last thing I needed, didn't I? Actually, the *last* thing I needed was a visit from the perkiest chorus girl in the entire theater world. A woman with so much enthusiasm, love of the art, passionate loyalty, and resounding *joy* that no one with an ounce of artistic temperament (read that: nerves) could stand to be in the same room with her for more than four minutes without a shot of insulin.

I focused. Concentrated. Professionalism overcame hysteria. I reasoned that as long as I had something close to clothing on my body, the audience would never know the difference.

"*Vic!*" the voice drilled through the back of my head. "It's Khaki! *Khaki*'s here *too!*" she trilled enthusiastically—the only way she knows how.

I stared hollowly into the makeup mirror and tried to remember my first line. All I could grab onto was "Well . . ." I tried to remember when my only fast change occurred. Two tiny, little arms enveloped me from behind.

A poof of aggressive blond hair wrestled (and lost) with my red. Lipstick smudged my cheek and was hastily scrubbed away, leaving a red blotch on my left cheek. Khaki was, indeed, there.

So much for the power of denial.

"*Five minutes!!*" the stage manager shouted at the same time he knocked twice at my door.

So much for my shower.

"*Thank you!*" Khaki shouted back happily. "Khaki can't believe we're going to be working together again. She was just saying during rehearsal that you were the best Miss Mona she's ever worked with!"

Another, shall we say, weird thing about Khaki is her inability to refer to herself in anything but the third person. Once you notice, it will drive you directly to the Prozac zone.

"Thanks, Khaki," I mumbled, concerned again about costuming, since worrying about lines was just too much for my frayed synapses. "By any chance, do you know what I'm supposed to be wearing, and when?"

"You mean Miss Mona?" she answered, and without taking a breath continued, "Well, of course that's who you mean. Of course Khaki knows. She's been rehearsing for *weeks*. And you know how she likes to be ready in case anything happens, and, of course, it *did,* but Jonathan explained to all of us how it would be easier to get you in here than to have to take in all these costumes for Khaki. I'm a size three, you know. Anyway, of course, Khaki understands that. The show's the thing, after all."

When does the woman *breathe?*

Khaki immediately started ripping outfits from the pole on which they were hanging and reorganizing them in proper position. Did I believe for even an instant that she would be setting me up for disaster so she could have the ultimate understudy wet dream? Dan would have brought up the possibility. Being a New York City cop has made him hard in many ways that are of absolutely no use to me.

Pardon my sarcasm.

But not for a second did I believe that Khaki would set me up to fall on my face. Well, maybe a second, but Khaki—beyond all her idiosyncracies—is, in fact, one of the more anal-retentive of theater people.

She really believes that the show is the thing. What specific thing, I have never asked. Alas, in professional acting, this does not earn anyone extra brownie points.

Khaki blathered on, "Don't you worry about anything. Khaki's onstage with you almost all the time and you know she knows everyone's lines. We're just so *excited* you're here. The house is sold out to the walls and the critics all agreed to come back again tonight. After all, it isn't that often that there's a *star* in the cast, in this part of Maine. Isn't it *exciting?*"

"Wow. Yeah. Thanks." I hoped that, in her exuberance, Khaki had not oversold my talents. That is the sort of thing one does for oneself while standing on the unemployment line or working as an office temp.

Knock, knock.

"Places!" I thought I was going to learn to hate the prepubescent stage manager's inexperienced little guts, and that was if he was lucky.

"Oops!" Khaki chirruped. "Gotta go. Khaki's in the opening." Another big, wet kiss, and mop up. "Break a leg!"

I wished.

I shoved my cheat sheet down the bodice of my dress—just as if there were any way I could pull it out of my bra and casually peruse it during a scene in front of two hundred witnesses—and took my position at the top of the stairs for my first entrance.

My heart was thudding so heavily I was sure I was going to suffer a myocardial infarction and not have to go on after all.

Having bad karma and all, this did not happen, and before I knew it I found myself standing in a newly repaired spotlight (pink-gelled, thank you, tech crew) and saying many of the words I was supposed to.

My first song started and ended without anyone on stage looking at me as though I was from Mars, as did the second.

It was a little disorienting to have to figure out which characters were which, just by what they said to me, but I don't think I screwed up too badly.

Sometimes *not* knowing who people are is much better than knowing. You know?

About the time into the play that I thought I just might survive opening night, Ed Earl—the sheriff and leading man—made his entrance.

To a deafening applause.

Make that *thunderous* applause.

Make that a stop-the-show, the-rest-of-the-cast-may-as-well-go-home-and-eat-worms, foot-stomping, whistling and screaming welcome.

I stood like a wart on an especially unattractive ogre waiting for the commotion to die down as I stared into the face of the tallest, handsomest, by-God humpiest man I had ever seen in my life. And I had seen plenty of him.

There were three years of him on videotape for insomnia nights; I had him on the covers of every lowbrow magazine to which I secretly subscribe. I had starred him in 80 percent of the manufactured, just-before-sleep fantasies I had concocted over the past five years.

This was no aging summer stock actor gleaned from an open cattle call in New York City. The audience was quiet.

My leading man waited uncomfortably for me to speak while I entertained the possibility that I had lost my mind somewhere back in New York City and was playing out this little scenario in some futon suite in the Hotel Silly. There was no other explanation for my sharing the stage with the hottest television star in the United States and Europe. For all I knew, Saudi Arabia, too. Six feet five inches of green eyes, dimples, sandy mustache, and broad shoulders. A smile that could light up the inside of a cow's gut. After thirty-ninish years, I was acting at *the* Nick Jacobs: *Jake Manley, Running Tough.*

"So . . ." Ed Earl/Nick Jacobs/Jake Manley prodded helplessly. His beautiful eyeballs were jiggling with fear. "So . . ." he repeated, looking into the wings for some nonexistent director to yell, *cut!*

This confirmed my suspicion that I would be acting *at,* rather than *with,* my co-star.

"Ed Earl!" I answered to a wave of laughter.

Fortunately for me and poor terrified Nick Jacobs, a good laugh from the audience is the ultimate verbal Ex-Lax. Lines spewed forth—in proper order, delivered deftly.

I am not bragging here; it is just that after fifteen years or so on stage I can tell the difference. It was also the first time out of five *Whorehouses* that I had an Ed Earl who was so undeniably boffable. If I had, indeed, gone around the bend, I figured to hallucinate with a bang.

So to speak.

By the climax to the first act, I was on a roll, and thoroughly enjoying my trip to la-la land. Insanity could certainly be worse than having it with Nick Jacobs.

Let's face it, being staked naked to an anthill with Nick Jacobs wouldn't be bad.

Khaki was already in my dressing room by the time I got there to change into my second act costume.

"You were wonderful! But everyone knew you would be. Khaki wouldn't want to speak ill of the dead or anything, but Garrett—she's the dead Miss Mona—well, she just didn't have the personality to carry it off. I mean, she was *good,* all right at least, and she was *way* bigger than Khaki, so we couldn't share the same costumes, but she wasn't . . ."

"Khaki," I interrupted with less grace than necessary, "why didn't you tell me that Nick Jacobs was doing Ed Earl?"

"She *did*. She told you we were sold out to the walls and that a star . . . oh." Khaki giggled—which she does. "You thought star meant *you*. Well, of course you're a star. Everyone knows it who sees you, but, I mean, not all that many people have seen you. You know?"

I knew.

"Is he in the next show, too?" I asked.

"Well, yes, of course. He's playing Macbeth, you silly."

"Take it back!"

"What?"

"You just said the M name in my dressing room. Quick. Go outside, turn around three times, and beg to be readmitted."

"What?"

"Just do it!"

Khaki scurried outside and performed her task. Against my better judgment, I let her reenter my den.

"Really, Vic, I don't see how we're going to do the musical without ever mentioning the names of the leading characters, do you?"

Actually, I didn't. But I would deal with that at a later date.

"So I'm superstitious."

"Oh, you silly. We're terribly excited. This is going to be the first musical version of Macbeth ever!"

"Out. Out, out, out, and twirl, Khaki!" Notice how I resisted the driving impulse to finish the "out, out" quote from that Scottish play. I mean, I am *really* superstitious about that particular Shakespeare curse. *"Out!"*

She did, and after begging reentry, I refused her entrance.

"Five minutes!" Knock. Knock.

"Thank you!" I yelled back, not being thankful at all. Khaki's double gaffe had made me nervous all over again. Great.

Despite my feelings of impending doom, the second act went as smoothly as the first—right up until the final number.

The cast members were gliding slowly into their positions on the dimly lit stage: cowboys and call girls on the upper staging, the final notes of my solo fading into the back of the room as I slowly walked across the set, covering furniture and taking a final look at the best little whorehouse in Maine.

Sobs resounded from the attentive audience, just the way they are supposed to, and I was exhilarated with having accomplished the impossible, when a bone-cracking snap followed by a heavy thud shot through the room.

Ever the professionals, none of the actors broke character, but we knew something had just gone very wrong.

During the several curtain calls, there was no sound of the piano coming from the band at the rear of the stage.

When we gestured applause for the orchestra, Jonathan was missing from his place at the piano.

It seemed an eternity before the curtain fell.

FIVE

DURING THE FINAL lights-out, I could feel the other performers whizzing by me, casting invisible swirls of hot air over my sweaty body. I was trapped in the darkness by my unfamiliarity of the set, listening to the shuffling, buzzing audience sounds during their exodus.

When the work lights came up, I was standing alone, center stage, eyes throbbing as they adjusted.

"Vic!"

I should have enjoyed my solitary moment. The irrepressible Khaki had re-Velcroed herself to my side.

"What happened?" I asked.

"The scaffolding let loose upstage. The railing just *collapsed*. Khaki's never seen anything like it. The rail is just *gone*. Just like *that*." She pointed behind me and, sure enough, there was a hole like a gap-toothed smile staring back at me where there had once been a security rail.

"Khaki . . . Khaki!" I twirled her back around to face me. "Was anyone hurt? Did someone fall?"

She tucked her chin to her chest in amazement at my idiocy.

"Well, of *course*. You must have . . ." I slid past her and out to the wings. ". . . heard the noise." She followed me. "It was Little Jon," she gibbered, "and it looks like he may have broken his *leg*."

And he might have. Amid the shattered wood, there was a splash of muddy crimson. But Little Jon was nowhere to be found. No one was to be found. Zip. Bupkis. Nothing but splintered two-by-fours and splattered blood. Had Khaki not been with me, it would have been positively surreal.

"Where's Little Jon? Where's Jonathan?"

"Oh, they're not here," Khaki explained, tucking a stray blond wisp back under her curly auburn wig.

"I can see that, Khaki, but where are they?"

"Oh, the producer, well, Charlie Mackin—he and his wife are both producers—you probably haven't had a chance to meet yet. You're really going to like Susan. You know, maybe she's as old as you are."

"Khaki! Come in, Rangoon! Where is Little Jon?"

"Khaki already told you. She knows she did."

"No, you didn't."

"She thought she did."

"Well, she *didn't*."

"She didn't?"

I don't know why people accuse me of having a short fuse.

"No, Khaki, you didn't."

"Well, if you say so." She shrugged very cutely. "Charlie took him to the Freeport Hospital Emergency Room."

"*Thank* you."

"Oh, you're welcome," she answered, oblivious to my

sorely tested self-control. "Now, you'd better change and get to the party. Everyone's waiting to meet you."

I allowed her to steer me to my dressing room, wondering what could happen next. I opened the door and immediately caught my elbow on a tuft of baby's breath, sending what must have been a rather lovely arrangement of red roses crashing to the floor.

The water from the vase splashed up the front of Khaki's industrial-strength pantyhose. Of course the glass shards found their way into my right shoe.

"Shit!" I fell one-footed into the beige folding chair at my dressing table, knocking a smaller arrangement of pink and white carnations onto its side and dousing my script with greenish water.

"Look, Vic, you got *flowers!*" Khaki kicked the broken vase under the table and leaned down to pick up the gift card. "Khaki bets she knows who sent you these!"

I inspected my foot. No damage. Another surprise. "Rush Limbaugh?"

"Nah-uh," she shook her head and held the envelope up the makeup lights. "Guess again."

"Oh, for *God*'s sake." I snatched the envelope from her perky little fingers with the perky pink nail polish and ripped open the edge. "They're from Barry."

"Told you so."

"Did not."

"Would have." Khaki tippy-toed around me and grabbed the envelope to the carnations. "And who sent *these?* Are you fooling around on your husband, Vic? Tsk, tsk."

Short fuse, indeed.

"Those," I took the card, "are from Rush Limbaugh." I

tissued off the majority of my stage makeup, removed the ribbon that gave me my Miss Kitty hair, and shook out the long rat's nest of red curls.

Stepping aside so that I would not drop my costume into the puddle of water, I peeled the perspiration-soaked spandex pants and red polyester blouse off my body.

"No, they're not. They're from *Dan!* Who's Dan?"

"Dan," I said, pulling a short white shift from my carry-on bag, "is my boyfriend." The dress looked wrinkled, but, then, so did I. I pulled it on over my head.

"You mean you *are* cheating on Barry?"

"Barry and I are separated," I spoke from beneath the sheer cotton.

"You're kidding!" She looked at my face as it emerged from the neck hole. "You're *not!* Oh, Vic, what a *shame.*"

"Yeah, yeah." I sat back down at the table and tried to reconstruct my face. "Since you're reading them anyway, what do the cards say?"

"Well, Khaki doesn't like to pry, but Barry says break a leg and he's coming in tomorrow to see the show."

"What?" I nearly poked my hazel eyeball out with the mascara wand. Khaki patted my arm.

"He still loves you, Vic. Khaki can tell."

I took a deep breath and leaned back toward the mirror.

"Yeah, yeah." I could sure tell *that* by the way he had cut back on his dating.

"And *Dan,*" her voice dripped disapproval, "says good luck and he'll see you Saturday."

"Good luck? *Good luck?*"

"Want me to take the card outside and turn it around three times?"

"*Good luck?*" A shiver shot down my spine.

How many curses do I need to get off to a really doomed start? Khaki came back into the dressing room from her turning the card around.

"You're going to need it, what with your *boyfriend* and your husband both being here on the same night." Oh, shit. Shit, shit, shit. "Really, Victoria, if Khaki didn't know you so well, she'd be *very* disappointed. Anyway, we'll see you in the green room, won't we?"

"Yes, we will," I answered, if only to prove I do not have a violent nature. I threw her the Zabar's bag containing the now warm and stale deli delights. Khaki, not being nearly as stupid as she behaves, took the opportunity to make her exit, admonishing me, "I hope that Rush guy won't be here, too."

I looked around the shabby dressing room. The spilled water and broken glass reflected tiny dancing lights on the stained ceiling. What a day.

What a night. I mopped up the best I could with paper towels. Like dressing rooms the world over, there were a dozen or more abandoned vases available for Barry's roses. I put the flowers at opposite ends of the table so that Dan's would not look undignified in comparison, and I sighed. A big, heaving, cleansing sigh.

So, I was in a dead woman's dressing room. So, my friend Little Jon was in the emergency room. So, the two men in my life were both going to be in the same one-lobster town on the same night. So, I was about to go into rehearsal for an adaptation of the most accursed theatrical piece in the history of civilization. So?

So, it was time for a shot of bourbon.

Maybe six.

★ ★ ★

Now, I have been to some parties in my day. This was not one of them.

The cast, unshowered and disheveled, was scattered around the green room, splayed over folding chairs, slumped on a musty old set sofa, and sprawled on the dusty floor. Beer bottles sweated into limp hands. Several pairs of eyes charted my entrance; several did not.

My eyes were hunting down a bottle of Maker's Mark, Jack Daniel's, Old Grandad, Thompson's, *anything* barrel-aged; all they took in was a case of Miller Lite.

I hate dancers; they are always on diets. Lite beer, indeed. Bourbon may be higher calorie, but at least it does not immediately bloat you.

No, sir. Bourbon is a clean drink. It is straightforward and, by God, American.

A forty-something attractive woman with short brown hair brought me a beer.

"Congratulations, Victoria."

"Thanks. Do we have any bourbon?"

"Sorry."

"Not as sorry as I am." I took a lukewarm swig and felt a little better. "Thanks everybody!" I called to the cast, because it is what one does.

From the rear of the room, Khaki's voice rang out, "Hip, hip . . ."

"Hurray!" the cast droned in unison, and made attempts to smile and wave at me, no matter how feebly. Apparently, my leading man was too exhausted to even make an appearance. Just as well. Objectively, I was pretty sure I looked a lot like the stuff they shovel out of bat caves, but still vain enough to care. A little.

"We haven't met yet," the brunette said. I looked at her closely to see if I could remember her from any time during the show. I couldn't. "I'm Susan Mackin."

"My producer!"

"One of them. Charlie's taken Jon to the hospital." She noticed my empty bottle and handed me another one. "Jonathan's with them." Every scrap of Zabar's droppings had already been devoured. My stomach snarled.

"Oh, good. I was afraid Jonathan went over the edge, too." That would have been much worse. "Is Little Jon's leg really broken?"

"No, no. I'm pretty sure it isn't. After twenty-five years in this business, I've seen a lot of injured dancers, and I think at worst, he's sprained. I doubt even that."

"But the blood . . ."

"Nosebleed." Susan finished off her own beer.

"Well," I said, "I'm glad Jonathan went with them. For a minute, when I saw the empty piano, I was afraid something had happened to him, too, and we'd be taking turns at the keyboard."

Okay, so I was also relieved that without my pit bull of a musical director in the building I could light up a cigarette. Never has a carcinogen tasted so heavenly.

"May I?" Susan asked, taking a cigarette from my case.

"They're menthol."

"I'm desperate." I lit the cigarette for Susan and leaned against a green wall. "So I guess you haven't heard."

I harumphed. "There's so much I haven't heard. What?"

"Jonathan and Little Jon aren't together any more."

"No!" I stood up straight in shock. The two Jons had been together for a decade, at least. I couldn't imagine one without the other—let alone the two of them apart and working together, "What happened?"

"You remember the Mayor?" Susan glanced discreetly over her shoulder in the direction of the swishy blond tenor I vaguely remembered from the show. One of those actors who felt the need of two last names. Simmons Cothron. Cothron Simmons. Simple Simon. I really did not care, except for Jonathan.

"Little Jon strayed?" I asked, knowing full well that it had to be. Jonathan had a tendency toward the monastic, despite his flamboyance. "When?"

"First day of rehearsal. Jonathan probably didn't have the chance to tell you. The show's the thing, you know."

There was that platitude again.

Bang!

The exterior door to the green room slammed against the wall with a crack that literally made my heart skip a beat. A collective sigh rose from the cast, leading me to believe that, whatever had happened, happened all the time.

Standing in the door was a tall, wiry man wearing military fatigues. His hair had been shaven nearly to the skull. The heavy muscle of his right forearm, strained with the weight of the olive drab kit bag, was tattooed. My mother warned me about staying away from soldiers, but (sorry, Mom) I recognized the Marine Corps emblem rendered in blue and black.

Though stunned, I was not struck silent.

"Yikes."

Susan handed me her empty beer bottle. "You can say that again."

"Who is that?"

"That's our tech director, Buck Sawicki."

"Yikes." Even his name sounded like a ricocheting bullet. "Let me guess," I whispered, "Vietnam was very bad to Buck."

"Twice. You're a psychic," Susan whispered back.

"I'd rather not discuss it." And wasn't *that* the truth. Buck cut a swath through the reclining bodies and made his way backstage, radiating hostility as would the sun—if the sun were really, really pissed off.

"Charlie must have called him about the broken rail. I'd better fill him in." As she opened the door to the stage, muffled "F" words spilled over the threshold from our friend, Buck the Truck.

I told myself I followed to thank Buck for the pink gels, but, let's face it, I was fascinated. I had not seen a ranting, dangerous person steaming around and wildly gesticulating for, well, hours. Not since I left New York. Frankly, I'd begun to think that the Big Apple had the franchise rights.

Buck had stripped off his shirt and was attacking the remaining rail with an ax. With each whack, he let out a deafening *"Arghhhhhhh!"* Susan stopped in her tracks.

"Oh, then, it's okay. He's rebuilding it."

"You're kidding."

"Arghhhhhhh!"

"No," Susan answered, "Buck believes that anything worth doing is worth doing right. He's just frustrated that something he built failed."

"Arghhhhhhh!"

"I'm awfully glad I didn't drop a line tonight."

"*Arghhhhhhhhhhhhhhhhhhhh!*"

"It'll be right as rain by tomorrow morning. Buck prefers working at night, anyway."

"Has anyone ever seen him in the daylight?"

"*Arghh! Arghh! Arghh!*"

Susan closed the door.

"Why, yes, I . . . very funny, Vic. Has anyone ever seen him in the daylight?" She smiled. "If you're up to it tomorrow, why don't we have lunch at the club? I could use some adult conversation."

The chorus was filing out of my celebratory party and marching sullenly toward the cast house, bellies filled with lox, bagels, and cream cheese.

"Well, it doesn't look as though I'll be hung over."

"Go on back to the cast house. I've got some paperwork to clear up, but I'll give you a call tomorrow—not too early—about lunch."

"Great."

Watching Susan shuffle away back toward the office area, I realized I didn't know the meaning of the word *tired*. The woman was exhausted. Of course, it was early in the season, and it's hard to hit your stride until you've gone over the edge at least twice.

Khaki met me at the door of my dressing room with my bags. I guess that constituted my going over once. Tears of wrung-out and burned-out actor filled my eyes, and I regained my composure without even really losing it. One more time over the edge and I'd be invincible.

Sure.

And the show's the thing.

★ ★ ★

I think there is a book of blueprints that has been floating around since the time of Euripedes that delineates the specifications for every cast house in the world.

The structure must be old—one hundred years, at least; the rooms must be small and dark—wallpaper absolutely required; the kitchen must not, under penalty of law, have a working coffee machine; and—this one is written in blood—under no circumstances whatsoever may there be more than two operating bathrooms, no matter how large the cast.

This house was a classic of its kind and a tribute to its type.

Khaki led onward and upward. She opened the door with a flourish.

"This is yours!"

Now, I may have been assigned the most claustrophobic room in the frat house, but it was a single. To say that nightmares of sharing a room with Khaki had been doing the Texas two-step through my head would be putting it mildly.

By the time Khaki and I had dumped my junk at the foot of what passed for my bed, there was no hot water left for a shower, but there was an empty bathtub, so I just counted both my blessings and immersed myself in the lukewarm water.

Oh. Did I forget the rule about no operating door locks, ever? No?

"Hi, Vic." Khaki sat on the closed toilet seat for a visit and some girl talk. I did not even open my weary eyes.

"Hi, Kak."

"Khaki has some great conditioner, if you want to use some."

"No thanks," I murmured. "I made a deal with my hair tonight. I leave it alone, and it leaves me alone."

"It's a little frizzy."

"It likes to be frizzy." I cracked open one eye. "Hand me a cigarette, will you, and tell me the poop."

"What poop?" She lit the cig, pulled a face, and handed it to me.

"Surely," I drawled, "you have noticed that this whole group and situation is weirder than, dare I say it, summer stock?"

"It'll be better now that you're here."

"Oh, puleeeeze. This is better?"

"Well, Khaki never speaks ill of the dead, but other people will tell you, so you might as well hear it from Khaki who will be a bit kinder." Khaki fidgeted with her little, tiny rings. "The old Miss Mona couldn't sing."

"Neither can the new Miss Mona."

She shook her head.

"No. You're untrained and undisciplined, and you *do* smoke, but you can sing. Garrett couldn't sing at all."

"At all?" That opened both my eyes.

"At all. Stone-cold tone-deaf. Jonathan had to have her speak her lyrics. Khaki offered to stand and sing behind the curtain and let her lip-synch, but she wouldn't hear of it. She thought she could *act* her way through. Well, not to speak ill of the dead, but . . ."

"She couldn't act her way out of a parking ticket, stark naked."

"Khaki didn't say it."

"Noooo. Why did Jonathan hire her?"

"Now Khaki doesn't . . ."

". . . want to speak ill of the dead, but . . ."

"But Garrett came as a package with Nick Jacobs." The

look on her face told me Khaki would never understand such behavior. And she probably wouldn't.

"Ah. And what the hell is he doing here at three hundred a week, when he has Hollywood chasing his perfect buns?" I believe Khaki actually appeared astonished at my naïveté.

"He needed some legitimate credits."

You'll have to forgive me; I hope Khaki did, but I guffawed. A long, healthy, raucous guffaw. My singularly raunchy laughter bounced off the peeling vinyl wallpaper, sparked off the rusty faucets, and ricocheted off the black hairy holes in the vintage 1950s linoleum. When I got control of myself, Khaki continued.

"He doesn't have any stage credits. You know how much the movie people admire stage work. It's the *craft*," she added with reverence. "It looks good."

"If you don't look too closely." I stood up. "Hand me a towel?"

"Didn't you bring any?"

How could I have forgotten. But I did. Summer stock means bringing your own linen. I reached over and grabbed my robe.

"Never mind."

"Vic, have you turned forty yet?"

I put on my robe.

"Why do you ask?" My solitary bed was calling to me.

"You still look pretty good naked. Especially for your age."

"Gee," I patted her cheek and pushed past her out the door. "Thanks, Kak."

"You're welcome," she called down the hall after me. "Really. She means it."

I closed my door and turned on the Roy Rogers table lamp next to my twin cot. It was one o'clock in the morning. I had not been awake for so many consecutive hours since dorm life. Of course, I had a better bed, then.

Rather than hunt through my luggage for a T-shirt to sleep in, I just threw on the cotton shift I had worn earlier. It would probably be chilly. Nonetheless, I shut off the light and immediately fell into a light drowse to ponder the meaning of life and the prospect of facing it all over again the next day.

The house was unnaturally quiet for a domicile sleeping no less than twenty-two people. Crickets and all those large and small Maine critters rustled outside my window. As a New England girl, I found every insect sound profoundly comforting.

A mammoth moth beat itself relentlessly against the torn window screen. The wind came up a bit and I imagined myself floating in a small, uncomfortable boat, waiting for the final descent into total unconsciousness.

Click.

Do crickets click?

No.

Click.

Moths most certainly do not.

Click.

A slash of light cut through the room from opposite the bed.

Kreeeeeek.

Crickets and moths most definitely do not kreeeeeek.

A large shadow muted the sliver of illumination. Someone was creeping into my room, and it sure as hell was no raccoon.

SIX

There are certain New York City Police officers who shall remain nameless (Dan Duchinski) who have regularly accused me of being braver—or at least more audacious—than I am smart.

I offer in my own defense the certainty that, had I not relieved myself before going to bed, I most assuredly would have relieved myself while observing the ominous shadow approaching me *in* bed.

I would like to say that I considered my many options in this, shall we say, distressing situation. I will not say it, because what I did was squeeze my eyelids tight and pretended to be asleep. Masterful plan, yes?

The door creaked shut again. Naturally, with my eyes closed, I could not be sure that my intruder had made his or her exit, so I opened them. Another brilliant plan gone awry.

The figure stood over my bed in the dull moonlight. I could barely make out what appeared to be a blunt object in the shadow's right hand as it leaned over toward my face.

With the lightning reflexes of a trained professional athlete, I leaped into action—or, at least, up from the bed like an over-the-hill dancer. Being less dexterous than most, I also inadvertently cracked my head into that of my stalker. Quite vigorously, judging by my would-be assailant's immediate dropping of the weapon and clutching of his or her face.

I was at the door within a second and pulled it open to reveal in the spilling hall light one bloody, wincing television star.

More confused than usual, I flipped on the overhead bulb and raced to where Nick Jacobs had collapsed on the side of my bed, bleeding rather profusely from his perfectly chiseled nose. I stood over him and frantically searched for something with which to defend myself.

The pervert. I know what all that sun in Los Angeles does to the brain.

Jacobs reached down to rearm himself, but (for a change) I was faster and ripped the cold, clammy instrument of terror from his powerful fingers.

"Champagne?" he asked from behind his left hand.

No slouch, attending to every detail, I checked out my weapon.

Sure enough. It was a maliciously chilled bottle of killer Dom Pérignon.

Blood dripped from between Nick's fingers and onto those famous, ginger chest hairs. Perhaps I had misjudged him. I had to admit, it was darned considerate of him to come to me shirtless.

"Oh, my God," I whispered more to myself than to my puckish higher power.

"Just call me Nick. Vic, honey, could you grab a washcloth out of that closet there before I ruin these fine designer sheets?"

"Yes. Why, yes. Of course, yes." I opened the closet door and immediately found a washcloth folded on a wire rack on the inside of the door. There was an embroidered *H* in fine celadon green. Needless to say, not standard S(ummer) S(tock) leavings.

Apparently, the late Miss Mona's belongings had not yet been sent to her survivors. The towels were arranged so neatly it made me cringe a bit to upset their order.

You have to understand that I am as stymied by obsessively tidy people as I am by the concept of cold fusion and the big bang theory. I don't understand the principles, but it impresses the hell out of me that other people "get it."

I supposed the late Miss Heinrich wouldn't mind my mussing her linens at this late date, and handed the cloth to Nick. It was a good thing that he knew where I could locate bathroom gear in my own room, because I couldn't have done it without him.

"I am *so* sorry. So, *so* sorry. You must think I'm a complete moron."

"I know you have a hard head there, that's for sure." He looked up at me with his signature green eyes, one of which I was sure would be black by morning. "Could you slop some water on this cloth for me? And while you're in the bathroom, grab a couple of those Dixie cup things. I didn't want to go down to the kitchen to bag glasses."

"Yes. Yes, of course," I answered, already on my way down the hall and the bathroom. I brought back two paper cups of water and very sodden washcloth. Handing Nick the two waters, I sloshed the cloth across his chest and—wow, what a chest.

I mean I've seen chests but . . . well, not for a *while*. I dabbed at his chin and cheeks. They were just stubbly enough, you know what I mean?—until he grabbed my hand and gave me one of the cups.

"Cheers!" he toasted and downed the water. I followed suit, figuring I had made quite enough social gaffes already. "The cups are for the champagne, darlin'."

Pop. Fizz.

Dom Pérignon spillage ran over the top of my outstretched hand.

"You're very forgiving, aren't you?" I asked with genuine awe. He poured himself a cup of bubbly.

"Yeah. And I also realize I was sneaking into your room in the dark. I'm a little surprised you didn't mace me."

"Nah, the biggest danger would be macing myself." I took an appreciative sip. "I'm not good with props. Just ask Jonathan."

"That why he calls you cow-woman?"

"No," I threw down the entire two ounces of champagne and held out my cup for more, "that's an expression of endearment. Now, why *were* you sneaking into my bedroom under cover of darkness?"

One corner of his unbelievably kissable mouth crinked up in a boyish, yet eminently humpable, smirk.

"Who wouldn't?" He poured for both of us. "Actually, I didn't know if you were already asleep. God knows, you could probably use some, but I did want to welcome you to the cast in a more festive manner than with a lukewarm bottle of lite beer."

"I appreciate that."

I did, but you should know that masculine charm makes me nervous. I am simply not used to it.

"Do my best, ma'am."

No doubt in my mind.

"Thank you. I'm sorry about, well, about Garrett. I never met her but everyone talks about what a fine . . ."

"Boy. Your Mama brought you up good and proper, didn't she?" He laughed at me—you know it did not bother me a *bit*—and got up to shut the door to the hall. "Mind?" he asked, holding out a cheroot.

"Welcome it," I answered, cracking the window and pulling my portable ashtray from my fanny pack. He lit my cigarette and then his cigar.

Two on a match. I could not for the life of me remember if that meant anything. Of course, when one is sitting on a cot with the sexiest man on earth, such things seem, at the most important, not a bit important.

We went on to our third Dixie-ful of Dom.

"You were really incredible tonight, you know that," he asked in manner I recognized as rhetorical. I grunted, which is my way of avoiding compliments I think other people feel forced to make. "No, no, don't do that." He put his long hand on my knee and touched his finger to my lips. "I didn't know what was going to happen onstage tonight. What you did was, to me, impossible.

"When I act on the series, we take and retake, stop and start, mess up and fix. You, well, wow. You know I cried during our final scene?" All the Y-chrome sincerity was making me antsy. He continued, heartfelt, humble. "Without glycerin tears? First time. I salute you, and thank you, ma'am." We toasted again. "I'm going to end up learning something, after all."

"Yeah. Get out of show business."

"I'll drink to that!" We did. "I hate all the sneaking around."

"Next time, just knock."

"You are a funny lady, you are, Vic. Yes sir."

I leaned back against the wall and tried to blow a smoke ring. Failed, naturally. I think my respiration was funny owing to the close proximity of supercharged pheromones in a tight space.

"You mean the press watching your every move?"

"I mean everybody. If I'd gone to the party tonight, everyone would be watching me to see how I was handling Garrett's death. Half would think I was grieving, the other half, gloating."

"Why would they think that gloat part?"

"Garrett stunk up the whole show. Here I'm trying to lay some legitimate credits onto my résumé. I'm nervous and inexperienced enough. I need some help out there, you know?"

"And you're man enough to admit it?"

I think that question was coy, something I pride myself on never being. All right, it was blatantly coy.

"You're sweet, you know that?"

"Not true." He leaned back next to me. I silently begged God not to let me blather. "I can document it," I blathered. It would be shallow of me to blame the alcohol and lack of sleep.

"And so beautiful." His eyelids dropped just an eyelash's worth, as though dazzled by my New York pallor. "I never expected a replacement woman to be so very, very beautiful." He blushed ever so slightly. Damn, he was good. "Makes playing your lover almost cheating. Too easy."

Damn my suspicious nature and low self-esteem. Of course, both had contributed to making me the dilettante ne'er-do-well I had so successfully become. Not conducive to deluding oneself, however. Damn. Damn. I stubbed out my cigarette.

"Aw, shucks, Sheriff. I'll bet you say that to all the schoolmarms."

There. That would teach him to compliment *me*.

"Get under the covers, baby," Nick ordered.

"I beg your pardon?"

No one calls me "baby." I had never been even the tiniest bit babyish—even as an infant. You can ask my mother; she'll go on for hours about how ungratifying it was.

"Under the covers." He stood up to his full, tapered, towering, bare-chested height. "We're out of champagne, and you're too pooped to pop."

That could not have been a double entendre, no matter how much I wanted to believe it was. I tucked my feet under the sheets, which Nick pulled up to my chin. I felt like a mummy having a hot flash when he bent over me and slowly brushed his lips and ginger mustache lightly across my cheek and down to my mouth.

My synapses were too stunned to fire, so my lips just sort of sat there on my face. Probably just as well. I get into trouble when they're attached to my hormones.

" 'Night, Nick, you smooth-talking son of a gun."

" 'Night, darlin'. Sleep well."

He closed the door behind him. I stared at the ceiling for what seemed the entire night. Two more weeks with that man, and I was going to have to be carried out of "lobster world" on a stretcher.

And Dan and Barry were both coming to visit in about twelve hours.

And I would have to try to remember all my lines again.

And I still had not called my sister.

I fell asleep in self-defense.

SEVEN

NOTHING GOOD CAN come of a day that starts with getting up in the morning. It is a truth, like gravity, Murphy's Law, or menstruation on honeymoons.

One of the worst things about morning is the clarity with which one sees how insane one was the previous night. It is as if a person wakes up perfectly coherent and then deteriorates slowly throughout the day until, just before sleep, anything seems possible. By the light of day comes a quick look in the mirror and a blast of reality.

"*Vic!!*"

I did not know where I was. I knew I would never in any delusional state own a Roy Rogers table lamp and I didn't have a brother, so I wasn't at my parents' house.

Slasher was not snoring from underneath the sheets, trying to push me out of bed, so I wasn't in my apartment.

There were no carbon monoxide fumes laced with diesel fuel wafting through my open window, so I could not possibly be in New York City.

"Vic! Telephone!!"

Ah-ha! A cast house.

"Vic Bowering!!!!"

A cast house—where?

Did not matter. Phone important, section of United States temporarily unimportant.

"Keep talking, whoever you are, I'm coming!" I yelled. Since Khaki had shown me directly to my second-floor room, I had not the slightest idea where the phone was located. Yes, another of the cast house architectural imperatives is that there never be more than one of any of the "T" machines. Those are: telephones or televisions. "I don't know where the phone is. Keep yelling and I'll follow the sound of your voice!"

"Come downstairs!"

I did. Barefoot, robeless, teeth unbrushed, I followed the phantom voice. One red ringlet had woven itself inextricably into my right eyelashes. I found either the kitchen or the elephant burial ground for unwashed dishes and empty beer cans. I took a wild stab.

"I'm in the kitchen!"

"Through the door without the doorknob!"

Which, fortunately, was a "push" door rather than a "pull."

"Hang a left by the piano and toward the front door!"

Eureka. The ever-decorative pay wall-phone plus faceless intern.

"Thanks," I took the phone and my vocal friend disappeared into an area bleating what sounded to be "Wheel of Fortune" somewhere in the dim recesses of the first floor. "Hello?"

"Vic, it's Susan. You up for lunch?"

I caught a glimpse of myself in the cracked mirror by the

front door. I vaguely remembered some reference to a novel by Agatha Christie.

Another look convinced me it would take some gestapo primping to achieve the status of bat guano. Oh, well.

A commotion from what I assumed was the common living room made it difficult to hear, let alone crap out.

"Sure. When?"

There was the resounding thud of something heavy hitting a wall over the cheers of the television audience. I recognized Little Jon's agitated shout. Susan continued, oblivious.

"You have rehearsal at two, so how about I pick you up in a half hour?"

I checked my face again in the hall mirror to confirm that I really was the disaster I had first thought. Sure enough. Little Jon came hopping around the corner, followed closely by whats-his-two-last-names, the show mayor.

"Don't tell me he didn't do it," Little Jon shrieked. "That railing failed because someone rigged it to fail. Don't tell *me* about staging!"

I cut my phone conversation short. I could not hear, anyway.

"Sure. See you in a half hour, Susan." Little Jon tried to grab the phone from my hand before I had even hung up. I pulled it back. "What are you screaming about, LJ? Are you all right?"

"All right? She wants to know if I'm *all right?* I'm lucky I didn't break my damned neck. That was probably the plan."

"What plan? What the hell are you yammering about?"

"Give me the phone. I'm calling the police." Little Jon twisted the handset from my fingers and punched nine-one-one. "Damn!" He hung up. "Who has some change?" The pretend mayor stood fluttering and helpless in the foyer.

"Are you trying to say," I persisted, "that someone wanted you to fall off the back of the stage?"

"No," Little Jon searched his shorts pockets for silver, "I'm trying to say that Jonathan was trying to kill me—or at least wreck my legs so I'd have to drop out of the show and we are so far out in the puckerbrush that there isn't even nine-one-one service!"

I almost asked Little Jon if he was kidding, except everyone knew that it was Jonathan—not his lover—who had the impish sense of humor.

All I could say, checking Little Jon's watch, was "I don't believe it."

"It doesn't matter what you believe," he countered. "You haven't been here, and I'm telling you that Jonathan would rather see me dead than with another man. And he sure as hell—may he rot in it—doesn't want to honor my contract to go anywhere near Broadway with *Oh, Mac!* Grow up, Vic."

I hate it when people tell me to grow up. If I am not grown up, where did all those crow's-feet come from?

Little Jon and his new friend stormed off, presumably in search of a quarter. I had already squandered six minutes of my precious resurrection time on the melodrama.

Now, don't think for an instant that I believed I would be able to look good in so short a time, but as a professional actor, I figured I could *appear* to look good in twenty-four minutes plus travel time. It's all done with mirrors and low lighting.

That's right! I was remembering *The Mirror Crack'd*. Elizabeth Taylor. Loved her. Wish I had the number of her surgeon.

No problem as long as I could find my way back to my room.

"Good *morning*, Vic," Khaki trilled. "Come watch 'Wheel of Fortune' with us. Did you sleep well?"

"How do I look?"

"Well," she answered, wearing her best poker face, "you can catch up on your rest tonight."

"Khaki, can you get me back to my room?"

"Are you *lost?*"

"*Khaki!*"

It was the blond leading the blind, but we made it. I unceremoniously tossed her from my space, threw on the first outfit I could locate from the top of my unpacked suitcase, leaned over and scooped my hair into a ribbon and pulled the curls over into the semblance of a "do," and grabbed my portable makeup case.

Abiding by the steadfast rules of summer stock order, both bathrooms were full, steam billowing from beneath the doors. I spread on some mascara and blush just as Susan drove up into the circular drive in front of the house. Lipstick was out of the question.

On the off chance that Nick Jacobs had actually kissed me the night before, I wanted to check later for trace evidence.

Susan did not seem to notice anything peculiar as I hoisted myself into the passenger seat of the white minibus.

Fortunately, the suspension was good, since I had some additional repair work to do on my face during the drive. It took about fifteen minutes—more than enough time for a patch job—of driving in the company van before we pulled up at The Club.

The mid-Victorian estate positively gleamed like a white grin at the top of a swell of broccoli-green lawn. The smell of salt water blew wetly from the east, though the day was clear and aggressively bright.

"Are we near the ocean?" I asked dimly, following Susan up the crushed stone path to the entrance.

She looked at me strangely and then seemed to remember that she was having lunch with an "actor," after all, and should not expect any coherence for at least another hour.

"Right over that crest."

We walked into a fabulous entrance foyer scattered with Oriental carpets and obsessively polished antique furniture in a dark mahogany finish. I wished I had worn heels, no matter how towering they would make me. It was that sort of decor. In truth, I was not much used to "decor." My apartment in New York just sort of happened.

I followed Susan through a less-formal sitting room and into what had once been a conservatory, but now served as the dining room.

Multipaned floor-to-ceiling windows revealed a startlingly decorative view of the Atlantic Ocean and a small huddle of ostentatious sailing vessels of the private variety.

Wow. If they had a smoking section, it was going to take a loaded .45 stuck directly to the freckles at my temple to get me to go back to the cast house. Susan addressed the scrubbed-pretty woman who approached us at the dining room entrance.

"Smoking, please," Susan requested.

I was going to love working with these people, despite the higher-than-average mortality rate among the grunt labor.

The tablecloths were crisp white damask with forest green squares arranged catty-corner. The napkins were paper, but, then, it was lunch.

"This is lovely," I understated.

My grandmother would have been so proud of how civilized I sounded. Susan smiled.

"Charlie's joining us. He's been looking forward to thanking you for bailing us out. He thought you were absolutely wonderful last night." Did that mean she did not, or was I just plunging into the icy waters of artistic paranoia? It has happened before, though I always deny it. Another very sparkly clean young woman appeared at our table, carrying a pad and pencil. "Wine?"

"I wouldn't dare," I said, though I sure wanted to dare. I had been through enough first rehearsals with Jonathan Resnick to know they were better faced ripped to the tits. Knowing that his long-term relationship had hit the skids did nothing to reassure me that the afternoon was going to proceed calmly. Jonathan "in a mood" was like being hermetically sealed in a Baggie with a hive of yellow jackets. "Iced coffee would be lovely, though."

Blechhh.

"Milk and sugar?"

My lips were forming the phrase "Nahh, a double-shot of Baileys," but my brain kicked in at the last minute.

"Black, thank you."

My grandmother would have been *so* proud.

Susan nodded approvingly and said, "Stoli martini straight up with a twist."

"Make that two," the tall, thin man behind me ordered and sat down. He had a cherubic face despite his fifty-some-odd years and a gangly charm. He offered me his hand. "Hi, I'm Charlie." His grasp was cold. Poor circulation, I thought. He must have been miserable during the frigid Maine winters.

"Nice to meet you at last," I answered.

I would like to report that my producers then launched into a love fest of admiration for my stellar stage presence and exceptional talent. Except they didn't.

"Buck called the police," Charlie grunted.

"He what?" Susan said.

"He what?" I echoed, trying to stay in the flow of conversation.

Buck Sawicki looked more of the kind of man whose photo was posted on the station wall than one who called to report. Probation, perhaps.

Charlie looked around as though he would prefer to have his martini shot directly into his arm than wait to swallow. He relaxed a bit at the sight of our waitress, hoisted his glass in a half-assed salute in my direction, downed it and ordered another.

"He told Chief Verenes that the rail that gave out last night was no accident." Susan shook her head in amazement and explained further to me.

"It's a matter of pride to Buck that he builds a set better than most people build houses. That's usually true. It takes us longer to strike some sets than it takes Buck to put them up."

"Yeah, well," Charlie said, already looking around for the return of our waitress, "I think he still blames himself for the wiring glitch that—where is my martini?—killed Garrett."

"Was it his fault?" I asked.

"No." Susan answered for her fidgety husband. "No. Absolutely not. It was an old outlet. No circuit breaker. Garrett just had the bad luck to complete the electrical circuit. The ground wire had never been connected." She looked at me for a reaction, which she got, however well-bred and understated. I closed my mouth relatively quickly. "Buck went right in and put everything up to the new building code."

Not much of a relief to Garrett Heinrich, I thought. And

what other minor oversights had my name written all over them?

"I can't stay," Charlie said and stood. "Cancel my drink, or finish it yourself or something. I've gotta get back to the theater before Little Jon starts ranting at Verenes. He accused Jonathan of rigging his accident last night. Between lovers' spats, electrocutions, and rehearsal, I'm going to have a nervous breakdown." That would do it. "By the way, Barbara, good show." He patted me on the top of my head.

Barbara?

"Charlie's not good with names," Susan explained. "Oh, my, look at the time. We'd better order so I can get you back for rehearsal. There wouldn't be much of a show without our Lady Macbeth, would there?"

There was that "M" word again. I forced myself not to spit between my fingers to counteract the evil eye.

At least not in public.

I ordered the lobster salad and tried to convince myself that superstitions were barbaric. Unfounded. Not rational.

Instead, I counted the "accidents."

Garrett unceremoniously fried—that was number one. Little Jon hitting the floor like a June bug on a windshield—number two. I almost hoped for a touch of salmonella in the seafood—a nice, benign number three.

No such luck.

The Hempstead Township Police cruiser was parked in front of the theater when Susan dropped me at the stage door, twelve minutes late. But, then, who was counting?

I sprinted in through the green room and opened my

dressing room door to dump my purse. An enormous floral concoction of Casablanca (my favorite) lilies hunkered in the center of the makeup table right next to a fifth of Jack Daniel's. The screaming from the stage beyond the lounge door distracted me from investigating at leisure.

"Sorry I'm late," I shouted before I even got through the scrim. Tripping over the prostrate form of a nameless dancer added to the allure of my entrance.

The principals were seated in folding chairs strung across the length of the stage, featuring an enormous void next to Nick Jacobs where my butt was, no doubt, supposed to be parked. As I had feared, Nick was sporting two not-so-natty bluish bruises beneath both of his sea green eyeballs.

The infamous Bowering karma had struck again.

"Well!" The keyboard cover of the rehearsal piano slammed open with a crack that let me know Jonathan had snapped the sounding board of yet another innocent Steinway. Younger members of the cast winced. "Her Majesty has deigned to join us." He threw a two-inch thick manuscript directly at my head. Fortunately it was bound. Also fortunately, Jonathan has lousy aim.

"I'm sorry, Jon, I . . ."

"I don't want to hear it. I don't want to see you right now. I don't want to *lose* my *temper.*"

Little Jon leaned back on his arms. "That would be a first."

"You," Jonathan glared at Little Jon, "shut up. Get ready for a sing-through of the opening, people. Bowering," he turned his attention back to me, oh joy, "get the fuck out of my sight until I call you."

The furious chords of the overture blasted from the tortured piano. No one would catch my eye, except Nick Jacobs, who lifted an eyebrow and mimed blowing his brains out. Smooth. My God, the man was smooth.

And I thought it was no longer possible to humiliate me. Life is just filled with surprises.

I slinked backstage, carrying my sheaf of 8½-by-11 pages, wondering why I ever thought acting was easier than honest work.

"Hey, watch it!" Buck barked at my poor, stooped personage. Too late, naturally, as I stumbled over the newly constructed and painted railing spread over newspapers on the floor. "Jesus H. Christ, woman. Do I look like I need this shit? I do *not* need this *shit!*"

Over the melodic strains of Jonathan's music I could hear him bellow, *"Shut the hell up backstage!"* without missing a note.

"Sorry," I mouthed, trying to look as unarmed as possible. This is a technique that works well for me in New York— except at Zabar's, naturally, where there is mercy for no woman, or beneath the withering stare of Buck Sawicki. Kindly hands steered me backward and safely through the rear loading door into the daylight.

My savior turned out to be someone even more unfamiliar to me than the relative strangers on stage. Overweight, medium height, freckled, topped with a stack of carrot-red hair—had I met him before, I would have remembered. Redheads always examine one another as the curiosities they are, even between themselves.

"Havin' a bad day?"

"You could say that. By any chance do you have a cigarette?" Why is it that the less one *should* smoke, the more one needs to?

"Quit," the man answered, shrugging. "One yea'h, three

months, fou-ahteen days 'go." How could I not like this man in the green drab uniform?

"You must be Chief, uh . . ."

"Verenes, ayuh. Rod to my friends. And you're . . . ?"

"Vic Bowering, known to my friends as Mud."

"Nice to meetcha, Mud."

Now, however homespun and comfortable Rod Verenes seemed to be at that moment, it did not escape my attention that this was the first time in my checkered history that I had ever met a police officer backstage at a theater. But, then, over the course of twenty-four hours, there had already been a series of firsts. Enter the antagonist.

"You see? You see?" Buck accused and slammed an armload of lumber into a pile six inches from my right foot. "Jesus H. Christ. Bunch of dipshits walking around with their . . ."

Verenes broke in. "Were you onstage last night?" he asked me.

"Shit, yes," Buck groused. "No rubber on her character shoes. Guess the hell I'll be sanding the crap out of the furrow she cut in the staging for the rest of the season. Jesus H. Christ. Must weigh a hundred fifty pounds."

"One thirty-five," I protested righteously, lying by only seven pounds.

"You the replacement?" Verenes asked.

"Yeah," I admitted without a lot of joy. "I'm the one."

"So you must have been at the theat'ah yesterday aftah'-noon getting ready, ayuh?"

"Ayuh," slipped out before I caught myself. "Yes, why?"

That niggly feeling I had been having was not salmonella, after all. Food poisoning can be barfed up; I knew I was stuck with dose of founded suspicion until it ran its course. I like the unfounded kind so much better.

My preoccupation was such that I paid no attention to the sound of wheels scrunching the gravel behind me. If Buck had not perked up like a Doberman, I probably would have ignored the whole matter.

The red Toyota with the New York plates was more than familiar. It was Dan Duchinski's. And seated beside him in the passenger seat was my not-very-long-lost almost ex-husband, Barry Laskin.

No matter what anyone tells you, wonders *will* never cease.

Both car doors slammed simultaneously, and the erstwhile Doublemint Twins sauntered toward me.

I know I asked before but, slow day, God?

"*Vic! Vic!*" Khaki whined as she careened into the sunlight. "*Vic!* Jonathan's having a *cow!* You'd better get inside in a *hurry!*"

Seemed like a sound idea to me. I looked from Dan's face to Barry's and then back again, made a stupid squeaky noise and allowed myself to be dragged from my own personal frying pan right into the fire.

The last I heard on my way back into the darkness was Buck Sawicki grunt, "Duchinski."

And Dan grunting, "Sawicki."

My higher power definitely needed a hobby.

Jonathan had calmed down some. Khaki was weeping silently into her tiny, little hands. Because I am not a very nice person deep down inside, I breathed a sigh of relief. When Jonathan is under stress, it does not matter much upon whom he vents his frustration. With me outside, Khaki caught the foulest of balls and I was, temporarily, safe.

There was only one more shouting match during that rehearsal. It stemmed from the physical impossibility of my singing a high A. In fact, I did not even try. In the finest tradition of Lauren Bacall and Bette Davis, I merely laughed aloud at seeing the heinous note printed on the page. Jonathan glared.

"Just try it! Again, from measure hundred fifty-six!"

I couldn't help it. I laughed again. In the proper key, though.

Of all the things that can kill, I am grateful that Jonathan Resnick's look cannot.

"I'm not fighting you, Jonathan," I explained, backpedaling furiously. "You know as well as I do that I *never* owned a high A."

Khaki chimed in helpfully, "Khaki could sing it *for* her from behind the scrim."

Jonathan glowered.

"Just take it down the octave, Bowering."

Never content, I pressed, "Could I take it down two?"

Nick squeezed the nape of my neck with the hand he had slung around the back of my folding chair and averted his face. I figured then that it was Nick who was my secret Santa with the whiskey.

Rather than enjoy the moment, though, it simply made me more suspicious. What would Nick Jacobs want with me? I am a good actor, sure, but I do not kid myself that I am any Meryl Streep. I have a certain appeal, but it is not Julia Roberts's.

"Fine," Jonathan answered in his best moderated voice. "Why don't we just have the two of you sing in the same *fucking* key?"

My self-abasement was interrupted by Mr. Mike, the adolescent stage manager signaling the end of rehearsal, no doubt saving my life.

There was no sign in the audience of either Dan or Barry. As usual, the men in my life had deserted me like wharf rats. The cast broke and nearly ran for the safety of the cast house.

"Vic," Mike called from the back of the house, "Charlie wants you to come to the office to sign your contract."

"Now?" I asked without much hope.

"Yep," the little snit answered. "You probably won't have time to eat before half-hour so you want me to leave you a sandwich in your dressing room?"

I looked at my watch. Sure enough, twenty minutes to half-hour.

"Thanks."

Nick kissed me on the cheek as he passed.

"I have real food hidden away. I promise you won't starve."

"Whole wheat okay?" Mr. Mike asked.

Oh, great. Not only would I be dancing around for two hours sloshing undigested food, there was a good chance that I would be regular, too.

I wondered what, besides champagne and real food, Nick Jacobs had stashed.

"Terrific, thanks."

I jumped off the four-foot stage and followed the worn carpet out toward the main lobby. To the right was the office area that, at one time, must have been horse stalls. The distinct odor lingered in the heavy air. Birds were squawking their final complaints of the day into the rustling leaves.

Suffice it to say, I lived through rehearsal, and I was trying to take a moment to be grateful.

The trouble with surviving summer stock rehearsal on a show day is that, in the process of memorizing new music, the stuff you learned for the show you are in the process of performing gets squooshed out of your brain like pus.

Nothing pretty about repertory theater.

From behind the closed Dutch doors to the office I heard Susan's voice.

"So we wait a year. It's only a year, Charlie."

"Sue," Charlie answered, "I know you're tired. I'm tired, too, but now is the time. We can finally make our dream come true." There was a sound of papers shuffling and a file drawer being forced closed.

"The dream will still be there next year, Charlie."

"But I may not be, Sue . . ."

"Stop it."

"We have to be realistic, Sue. The kids are grown. They don't want any part of this. We're both getting older and we deserve this chance."

Now, everyone knows how discreet I am under normal circumstances. Well, okay, *some* people do. I just wish I had the luck to live under normal conditions. Somehow I had inched my way nearer and nearer to the office door. Some little indiscreet scritch in my nature had leaned my better ear at the crack.

Of course I was simply waiting for a lull in the conversation so that I could announce my presence and sign my contracts. The unexpected opening of the door landed me a rather impressive smack to the right temple.

"Wow!" I yelped.

"Oh, no, oh, no, are you all right?" Charlie asked, obviously searching his database for my name.

"Wow. Oh, wow, wow, wow, does that hurt!"

Susan dashed to my side carrying a first-aid kit.

"Are you cut?"

"Only to the quick," I answered, rubbing tears from my right eye. *"Wow,* does that hurt." Susan inspected my face.

"Think you're going to have a shiner, Vic."

I cocked my head. "Another excuse to sparkle on stage." I touched the rising bump. "Some people will do anything to steal focus."

"Come into the office and sit down, Vic," Susan offered. "Charlie, you'd better catch a little nap before showtime." He nodded in a distracted manner, took another look at my blossoming black-and-blue, and wandered away.

The office was decorated in leftover set dressings: a mishmash of old show furniture shoved into whatever space was available. The desk was littered with computer printouts and Playbills—but the chair was comfortable and welcome. I was not exactly seeing double, but I have had better vision after two trips on the Super Duper Looper at Hershey Park.

"You need me to sign the contract." I smiled through my pain. I'm like that, sometimes. Susan started digging through the papers on the desktop.

"You'll have to excuse the mess." She dug deeper. "Charlie and I were just going over the books. Seems like that's all we ever do. Now, I know I had your contract right here."

"Can I help?"

Susan started making teetering piles.

"You have done more than we could expect already, Vic. Honestly," she looked as though she might have found what she was looking for, but then wadded the paper into a ball and tossed it at a full-to-the-top trash can, "if Jonathan hadn't found you, we would have had to close the season."

"Boy, would I like to believe *that*."

"Believe it. Maybe you've heard, Charlie and I are negotiating for two more theaters. One in Florida, one in Chicago. If everything works out the way we hope it will with *Oh, Mac!*, there's going to be more than enough work for everyone for a long time."

Now, that was music to my ears. I began to sort out what looked to be stuff with numbers from handwritten stuff from publicity stuff from contractual stuff. Nothing with my name appeared.

Oops.

I accidentally found out that Khaki was my understudy for *Oh, Mac!* and that she was earning a grand total of $175 a week plus a meal a day. This did not give me great hopes for what I was going to be paid.

Susan leaned down to pick up some papers from the unfinished pine floor as I (oops) accidentally searched for other contracts that might reassure me that no matter how little I was to be paid that it was more than anyone else.

You do not need to tell me that this is petty. It is very petty. But for a working actor, it is often all we have to cling to.

An official-looking document caught my eye at the corner of the desk, so I accidentally picked it up for a closer accidental look.

In my narcissistic "me-first" mode, I almost dismissed it when I saw Buck Sawicki's name typed at the top of the page. Techies always get paid more than actors. I accept it on the basis that they work harder than we do, but I don't *like* it. Still, it wouldn't hurt to know how *much* harder Susan and Charlie thought that Buck worked, so I held the document far enough away from my eyes to read the small print. No need. The big print was more than enough.

It was a parole report.

Buck Sawicki was on parole from the Maine State Prison on the charge of assault and battery.

"*Got it!*" Susan said from beneath the desk.

I dropped the report and leaned forward in an act of such overdone innocence that I could have been drummed out of the American Federation of Television and Radio Artists. You'd be amazed at how few people notice, though. Susan Mackin, for example.

"Here you go, Vic. We can pay you two thirty-five a week, plus fifty for rehearsal week, plus room and one meal a day. Just sign here and fill out the IRS forms and get it back to me sometime today or tomorrow."

Two hundred eighty-five dollars a week and the government was going to take out *taxes?* I signed the contract.

"Oh, and here are the Maine state withholding forms, too."

Maine, *too?* As far as I could tell, Maine was not spending all that much money that they needed some of mine.

"And get me your travel receipts, so I can cut you a check at the end of the run."

And I'm paying interest on my credit card for my plane tickets?

There was a knock on the wall.

"*Half-hour!*" Mr. Mike screamed.

"Thank you," I called, gathering my governmental forms and wondering why I ever left my lawyer-husband. Then I remembered.

He left me.

To work a $285-a-week job, less taxes and taxes and taxes. With a convicted felon. Replacing a dead woman. Getting kissed by Nick Jacobs.

Let's face it: I could do a lot worse.

Let's face it: I usually do.

My brain swirled with the infinite variety of life on the road and . . .

What *was* my first line?

EIGHT

For those of you who personally know professional actors, here's a little tip. No matter how much they beg you to come and watch their show, silently they are praying that you won't be there. If you are a casual friend, swell. That's fine. But if you are, say, an ex- or future-husband type, send flowers and wait for the videotape. Not that I was nervous that night, but I did manage to forget my opening line.

It was probably all that squinting I was doing to try and see into the audience so that I knew where Dan and Barry were sitting that made me blank out. Like the laser light on a state-of-the-art assault rifle, I could feel four specific eyes boring down on me, taking aim, ready to fire.

In deference to time and space, I will not go into how many different and inventive ways terrified chorus girls can exclaim, "Miss Mona!" "Well, hi, Miss Mona!" "Miss *Mona!*" "Miss Mona?" "Yo!" while Miss Mona stands there like Lot's wife, caught up in her own salty personal drama.

About the time I pulled myself back together, I realized that my fellow cast members were looking at me more strangely than usual. That was just before my swollen eye completely closed and reminded me how I must have looked.

When Sheriff Ed Earl made his entrance and he and Miss Mona faced off for their first scene, it was all Nick and I could do to keep from breaking down in childish giggling.

From close up, the show was beginning to look like "The Best Little Bell-Ringers in Notre Dame." So much for the theory that an actor's first obligation is to be better-looking than his audience.

There is another theory that, after a spectacular opening night (even the second opening night), the next show will suck. Ticket buyers beware. It is all true.

The timing was off during the dynamic and sexy clog dance done by the chorus boys. Little Jon did one of his highly touted midair twirls, landing his cowboy boot directly in the groin of his new lover. Jonathan Resnick's laughter could be heard all the way through the reprise. The hammer of my shotgun caught on my feather boa and would not fire, so I had to yell "Boo!" at the faux rabble-rousers trying to close Miss Mona's house and hope that the doubling chorus people would figure out what had happened. By Ed Earl's final number, "Good Old Girl," everyone just wanted the show to be over.

Nick strode into the spotlight for his tour de force song. I was backlit as a shadow, telling my girls that the party was over as the male chorus harmonized and set the bittersweet mood. I confess my mind was wandering to exactly how I was going to spend the postshow hours with Dan and Barry. Oh, and Nick, who was singing amazingly well for a TV guy having a bad night.

Crckkkkk. A staticy, high-pitched sound ground down the

small hairs of my neck. It was not loud, but of that pitch that brings forth images of elementary school and blackboards. *Crckkkkkk.* Pop.

Out of the corner of my eye, I saw Nick grasp the small of his back. His well-defined pectoral muscles stretched at the country plaid of his tapered shirt. The chorus came in, hesitantly, and then in full voice.

During the bridge, Nick pulled the body mike out of his belt, strode pensively stage right, and tossed it backstage, as though he were looking out at the sunset.

Pretty good, there, poopsie. Casual. Audience never knew anything even happened.

Nick made strong eye contact with the audience and walked downstage. Charisma in action; I could feel the audience connect like Nick was the plug and the house was the outlet.

Just before it was his turn to sing solo again, he reached down and casually grasped one of the manual mikes from the stage apron used to boost the overall sound of the action.

My guess was that Nick's body mike had gone out, so I double-checked to make sure mine was turned on, thunked it once with my forefinger and was reassured that I was "on." It would be just my luck to be singing my brains out, weeping real tears for the edification of my public, and then find out that no one could hear me.

If I was going to allow my nose to run in a tight spotlight, I wanted the full admiration quotient.

To my relief, I got it. During the curtain call, Nick unexpectedly polka'd me twice around the stage and then swung me up into his arms—to the delight of all but two (I assumed, no doubt correctly) of the audience. As I hugged Nick and clung for dear life during the third curtain call, I saw the wound.

It was small, about an inch, at Nick's belt line, but liquid was seeping at the perimeter, causing a wet stain to bleed evenly in a four-inch circumference. His shirt was evilly scorched at the center.

During the blackout, I heard Nick moan as he gently lowered me to the stage. He did not let go of my arm. In the darkness I whispered, "Nick, are you all right?" I felt actors brushing past us. The smell of clean sweat was everywhere and, faintly, charred fabric. As the work lights came up, Nick let go of my arm.

"Peel this shirt off me, will you, baby-cakes? I'm feeling like the main course at a luau."

"Unbutton your sleeves if you can and loosen your belt," I said. "The shirt looks pretty stuck and I don't want to hurt you any more than I have to." I came around and behind him as he did as he was told.

"Yeah, yeah. That's what my first wife said."

I could hear the last lingerers in the audience moving away from the closed curtain and away to the foyer doors. Carefully, I pulled Nick's shirttails out of the sides of his pants. The middle section was stuck to his skin as close as a wet suit.

Squinting through my one good eye, I reassured him. "This is going to hurt you a lot more than me, buddy-boy."

"That's what my second wife said." Nick's shoulders tightened as I started to pull the fabric away from the weeping sore.

For about the first time in recent memory, something was not as bad as it initially looked. Dead center in Nick's back was a raw circle surrounded by singed ginger hairs. As burns will, it was seeping clear liquid, which was what had caused the shirt to adhere.

"Oh," I breathed with some relief, "that isn't so bad."

"Yeah, yeah," Nick started, and I joined, "that's what my third wife said," we finished together.

"Where's your body mike? It must have shorted, or maybe the battery leaked."

"Wasn't no goddamnit leak," Buck yelled from the wings as he stormed through the black-gauze scrim. Perspiration gushed from his every pore, making the tattoo on his forearm glisten. Dangling from his fingers were the burnt and mangled wires of Nick's body mike. "I change those bastards every three days so I don't have to listen to no goddamned lip from no goddamned actor. This baby was cross-wired."

Dan Duchinski barreled his way through the green room door, Barry in tow. Both men looked as serious as surgeons preparing to attempt delicate brain surgery. Dan had the cannibalized remains of the mike case in his big paw.

"And it gets better, Vic," Duchinski muttered, handing me the electronic carcass. "What does it say here?" he asked, pointing out the label penned in red nail polish on the side of the mike.

"Miss Mona," I answered with barely a glance, as I reached behind my back to unclear the microphone I had hidden under my polyester blouse. "And I have Ed Earl's. My God," it hit me, "if I had been wearing my own mike, this outfit would have melted down like a nuclear reactor."

Barry sprang into action.

"You haven't signed a contract, have you?" he asked.

"I need a drink," I answered coolly.

I just hate it when Barry asks me a question to which he already knows the answer.

★ ★ ★

The "cocktail lounge and grille" was hopping and just a short drive from the theater. Walking distance, I noted, in case of dire emergency. Chief Verenes was already sitting at the bar when we arrived. All of us. Every single one, including Buck Sawicki and the two-member Vic Bowering Fan Club. It was that kind of night.

On my way to the ladies' room, I called to no one in particular, "Order for me and make it a double."

Had there been a mirror in the washroom, I would have neurotically checked my black eye, so it was just as well that we were all parked in a no-frills bar. I did note with satisfaction that there were exactly double the number of toilets as there were at the cast house and wished I had more business to do. Ah, well. I swished my way out and back into the noisy room.

The cast had appropriated five large tables and pushed them together, no doubt annoying the hell out of the poor waitress who was going to have enough problems keeping her eyes off Nick for the rest of the evening. As I approached the head table, Dan, Barry, and Nick stood as though they had been handcuffed together. Charming. Really.

In front of the empty chair onto which I placed my weary butt were six glasses. Two Bombay martinis—extra dry with olives (Barry), one red and one white wine (Dan), and two tumblers of Maker's Mark bourbon—one on the rocks, the other neat (Nick).

And I was feeling unloved.

Go figure.

Three sets of eyes bore into me to see which glass I would lift. Maker's Mark neat won. I threw it down in one gulp. Dan raised a disapproving eyebrow.

"You know how you get," Dan admonished. Nick leaned back in his seat, enjoying whatever the hell was going on.

"I know exactly how I get." I swallowed the white wine as a chaser and looked at Barry. "I get promiscuous on Bombay martinis. I get cuddly on bourbon, and I get acidosis on wine of any color." I picked up the bourbon on the rocks and sipped snidely, if that is possible.

It would have been apparent even to a blind belter that I had entirely too many men sitting around me to wreck my stomach with martinis. It had been so long since I had gotten lucky, I was not sure I would even know how.

"You signed the contract, didn't you, Vic?" Barry asked, not to annoy me, but because he just couldn't help himself.

"Of course she did," Dan answered for me. "You should know that better than me. Little Miss List-maker. You'll find out about that later. The Queen of Leap Before You Look." I took a healthy swig of bourbon. "And no power on earth will get her to back out of a contract. Oh, no. Not Vic. She is *such* a Republican."

"Righto," I agreed after sucking the remaining Kentucky mash down to the ice cubes.

Nick raised his hand to order me another. Since the waitress was hermetically sealed to his side, the order was placed in record time. I picked up one of the martinis.

"And what," Dan asked, the color rising in his bull neck, "would you say, babe, if I told you that your tech director is a psycho?"

"I'd say he'd be the right man for the job."

Nick laughed out loud and rubbed his chin, his eyes never leaving mine.

Barry chimed in his sheckel's worth.

"Vic attracts psychos."

"Oh, *no* comment," from me.

"Well, this one has a felony record," Dan shot.

"What?" Barry asked. "For what?"

"You name it. Assault and battery, concealed weapon, unregistered firearm, possession of a controlled drug."

"Wait a minute," I may have slurred just the tiniest bit before chewing my olive, "how do you know all that, Dan? I knew about the parole, but . . ."

"You *knew?!*" Barry was sputtering. I like that in a man. Nick handed me another bourbon, albeit heavily cut with branch water.

"I accidentally saw the report in the office," I said innocently and smiled warmly and, yes, maybe just the slightest bit promiscuously at Nick.

"Yeah, and I accidentally served with Buck in 'Nam." Dan grabbed the extra martini and dropped it down his throat without masticating the olive. Not a good sign from Big Dan.

"Curiouser and curiouser, said Alice," Nick piped from the opposite end of the table. I wondered how he would look stark, buck naked and decided to distract myself.

"I'm calling my sister," I said and excused myself from the table. Nick handed me a quarter as I brushed past him and the waitress who was still super-glued to his back. My luck, being what it is, meant that the pay phone was at the end of the bar right next to where Rod Verenes and Charlie and Sue Mackin were deep in conversation. Luck gave me a small break for a change. My sister's number was a local call.

Rather than allow me to be lulled into a false sense of security, the gods prevailed and I got her answering machine—upon which I left something that was, for the most part, incoherent, but included the name of the theater so that she could track me down in her ever-so-organized fashion.

My sister is three years younger than I, but was always the "smart, pretty one." The kind of woman who butchers her own venison and runs the school board. You know the type. I love her more than chocolate despite her perfection.

It is just possible that I missed the phone and the disconnect as I walked back toward the table from hell. Anyway, Rod Verenes hung up again for me.

"Are you all right?" he asked.

"Sometimes," damn that Bombay martini, "I am *excellent*. How are you?"

"It's all right, Rod," Charlie said, "I'll drive the cast back in the company van." Verenes nodded. "Barbara . . ."

"Vic," Susan corrected kindly.

"Vic," Charlie went on without embarrassment, "the Chief thinks it might be a good idea if we canceled the season. We don't want that, of course. It would ruin us, but I want to let you know, and you can tell the rest of the cast that, given, well, the things that have happened, we won't hold you to your contracts."

"Really," Susan confirmed, holding her husband's hand, her eyes red-rimmed.

"Aw." Drinking also makes me revoltingly sentimental. "I wouldn't dream of leaving." Stupid, but loyal. Then, naturally, the clincher. "Show must go on."

Verenes dropped a cardboard cylinder into my hand and pressed it closed. I looked down. It was a shotgun blank, toilet paper poking from around the metallic cap.

"You're lucky the shotgun jammed t'night," the Chief said. "That blank was so ovahloaded it would have exploded in your face—or at least set you on fi-yah."

"But Little Jon takes care of props, and, for a dancer he is *very* careful." I tried not to screw my face up too much, but I was flat-out scared. "Little Jon would never hurt me."

"He denies making this shot up for tonight's show." Verenes looked disapproving. "Said he was too busy."

I wondered if the poor light kept my producers and the cop from seeing how green I had become.

"Accidents happen," I mumbled.

"I cannot guarantee anyone's safety," Rod warned. Concern had marked his baby face around his lips. "This last business puts everything way over the edge of cursed shows and clumsiness. Something is happening at the theater that isn't, whatcho New Yawkers say, kosher?"

I recognized the serious look on the police chief's face. With or without freckles, it was the same stare Duchinski gave me whenever I was about to put my butt in a sling. I thought it was very sweet, but, then, I was gazoshed.

"Nah," I answered, "you don't understand how powerful the curse of Macbeth is."

Yikes, wow, shit, and damnation. Right out of my mouth it fell. Right *out,* just like that. No slur or hiccup or anything to dilute the doom that was going to fall as surely on my head as humidity on a talk show day.

"Excuse me," I bolted out the door of the bar. I turned around three times, and then three times more just to be sure, which upset my overwrought stomach to the point where I, with great delicacy, barfed into a juniper by the door. Oddly enough, I felt much better. When I begged reentrance to the bar, Susan immediately waved me in and explained the whole process to a very confused Rod Verenes while I sloshed my mouth with water.

In fact, my higher power had saved me from what surely would have been the mother of all hangovers. I was still gassed, but not obnoxiously so, and steadily made my way back to the cast. Nick, Dan, and Barry were clutched in conversation.

It was the sort of scene that only Neil Simon could do justice to. They stood in unison at my arrival. Three sets of hands pulled out my chair. Had they not been so damned handsome, I would have been thinking, Larry, Curly, and Moe. But, jeez, they were all *so* handsome.

"So, where you boys staying?" Nick asked.

The "boys" comment was not wasted on Dan, but whizzed past Barry as would a Boeing 747.

"We managed to get a room at the bed and breakfast down the street from the theater," Barry answered.

"We?" Sometimes I just can't help asking a question that I know the answer to which is going to disgust me.

"Just one night," Barry continued. "We thought if we could get along on the six-hour drive, we could get along for one night."

"Waste not, want not." I smiled, maybe tensely, I do not quite remember, and took a moderate sip of bourbon. I turned to Nick who was watching me with very sharp eyes. "Charlie and Susan said they wouldn't hold us to our contracts if we wanted out. Chief Verenes has recommended that they close the season."

"Great!" Barry approved. "You can drive back with us tomorrow morning. There's room. Assuming you don't have too much luggage."

Dan frowned. How he can know me so much better than a man to whom I was married for ten years, I will never know, but he does.

"Oh, don't worry about that, Barry," I crooned. "If worse came to worse, you could always just strap me to the hood like a jacked deer."

"She's not leaving," Dan said—sagely, if I may say so.

"Now, Vic," Barry led with his chin, "we all know how you can get . . ."

I stopped him with a truly frightening look that I have perfected over the years of being harangued on the streets of New York.

"Well," Nick interrupted, "I don't. Vic, darlin', how *do* you get? I mean, without the martinis? Everybody knows how you get then, but, say you were a brilliant, beautiful full-grown woman, how would you get then?"

There are moments in time when all the molecules in the air, furniture, and living things have the opportunity to zig, or zag. These moments are caused by something scientific and I would not dare to offer a clinical explanation, but I know it is as true as that if Slasher barfs somewhere in the apartment, it will be the first place I put my foot in the morning. I know it with acceptance, however dour, because it is just *true*.

These moments are inevitable, since the universe is infinite. The outcome, however, is not predestined. Any number of variables can change the most concrete of zigs right into the most serendipitous of zags. Usually, I enjoy observing the very weirdness as the moment unfolds. Because, bless me, I *can* still be surprised.

Unfortunately, I no longer derive pleasure from watching exactly what I expect to unfold.

It makes me tired. It makes me sad. It makes me feel so irretrievably female.

"I am not going to beat a dead horse here, Vic," Dan stated predictably. His eyes darted to Barry. I wondered what Dan knew that he didn't want Barry to know. Well, he should have thought about private time with his woman before he signed up with his new roomie.

"There is no point in discussing this when she's being, well, you know, like she gets," Barry agreed. My leg that was crossed at the knee started its predictable tattoo, twisting discreetly at the ankle beneath the table.

"Boy," I said, "are you guys smart. I will just never figure out why I don't listen to you. Why do you think that is, huh? Oxygen deprivation in utero? Recreational pharmacology during the sixties?"

"Don't get like that, Vic," Barry warned. "We are only looking out for your own best interests." Dan had the brains to keep his mouth shut.

My guess is that he can recognize those molecular moments as well as I and found himself powerless, sucked into his own morality like a mastodon in a tar pit. Wanting desperately to echo Barry's words, but too world-wise to give in to the urge.

Nick nodded in my direction and moved himself to an adjoining table. Privacy. Terrific. Just what I needed. If only there were such a thing as privacy ménage à trois.

But there isn't, and I was emphatically à trois.

"Go away," I whispered. The rocks glass in my hands was warming, and condensing water ran down my arm. I put the glass down carefully and lit a cigarette.

Barry had caught some vibes from somewhere, though

they were as foreign to him as a Bulgarian in a McDonald's.

"I thought you quit." He gestured to the cigarette.

"No, Barry. You wanted me to quit. I guess you are just confused. Now, if you two don't mind I would like to sit here, give myself cancer, an ulcer, and ruin my life in peace." I blew a gust of smoke skyward, not willing to give *them* cancer. "You know how I get."

I have only seen Dan so deeply, intestinally rigid once before in my life. And, of course, it was my fault. The two men shook their heads like the Bobbsey Twins and got up from the table. I did it. It was my fault. Only Barry looked back, and then only once. Every molecule in the smoky room whirred and collided.

That is how I "get."

I pushed the watery whiskey away, and held on to the glass of red wine as if it could keep me bobbing above the free-floating misery I felt. Nick slid himself back to my table.

"Woman, how do you do it?"

"Now what have I done? If you don't mind my saying so, I think I have filled my quota of mea culpas for the rest of the year." The wine in the glass looked bloody and tasted sour in my mouth.

Nick leaned in so that our shoulders touched. "How do you make men love you that much? And then," he crushed out my cigarette and lit two cheroots—one for him and one for me, "when they love you so much that dying would be easier for them than living with it, how do you make them hate you for it?"

"I am not going to cry, you shit."

Which of course I did.

"Let's walk back to the house, baby. It's going to be all right. I promise."

And, perfect asshole that I am and always will be, I believed him.

NINE

There were no cars or trucks wheeling past us on our cigar-chomping walk back to the cast house. Mainers, being the sane type of Americans—early to bed and early to rise. They work hard and do not overdo their entertainments. Though we did not speak a word over the mile or so toward "home," Nick kept his right hand pushed up under my hair at the nape of my neck for the entire walk, massaging it in a brotherly manner from time to time just to remind me that he was there.

Like I could forget it.

The tears that slopped over my waterproof mascara stopped almost the moment they started, so there was no atmosphere-shattering snuffling along the way.

Even though I knew better, I used the time to think.

Oh, nothing to save the earth or feed the children, mind you. I know my own limits. I was thinking about men.

Yeah. What a shocker.

I blame my dad for a lot of my problems with the opposite sex. He raised me as the son he never had, so I am comfortable in the company of males. They do not intimidate me, as a general rule, which is pretty silly since I seem to have a real knack for annoying the hell out of them. Which, naturally, makes me annoyed with them—particularly when they just flat-out refuse to tell me what I want to hear. That would account for approximately 99 percent of the time.

So, even though I can relax and hang out with the guys, it usually results in bringing out the prickly part of my nature. I am okay with this since it seems to be a fifty-fifty proposition. No foul, no harm. I am relatively content with the situation.

Ah, but those rare, few men who not only know exactly what I want to hear, but are ready, willing, and able to tell it to me, frighten the shit out of me.

Which probably proves that I am not nearly as stupid as I think I look.

And for those men of you out there: in a nutshell, that is why nice guys finish last. It's because we women are so put off by failing to get what we want that we cannot believe it when we're really getting it. That means we believe the liars and mistrust the trustworthy.

Or so I was thinking on that walk home that second night in Summer Stock.

Sunday was a matinee day plus twilight show, which meant that the cast had decided in its lemminglike way to drink themselves sick and walk through the two o'clock show, depending upon youth and adrenaline to get them through the second. It is not admirable, but it happens all the time. We had a full day of rehearsal on Monday, so Sunday evening was reserved for going through the motions and falling into a stupor of exhaustion.

In other words, the cast house was as empty as my bank account when Nick and I arrived. Both of us were stone-cold sober and wide awake. A nasty combination, I'm sure you would agree.

The mosquitoes were having their own bacchanal using our blood for their favorite vintage, so, as much as I would have liked to swing on the glider on the front porch, it was out of the question.

At the front door, Nick gave me a tight, lingering hug of comfort—sort of like high-school dating only without the skin eruptions.

"I have some good cognac if you're up to a nightcap."

"How good?" I do like good cognac.

"VVSSOOPP. I have it hidden."

"You must, or there wouldn't be a "P" left of it."

"Come on," he led me through the door, "this is probably the last time this house will be quiet for the rest of the summer. And," he added with a suave tilt to his head, "I happen to have a tape of *Robin and Marian* all keyed up on the VCR."

"There's a VCR? Noooo."

"Nooooo. I have a VCR. It's hidden right next to the cognac."

"Robin and Marian? Really?"

I should have been terrified at that second, because, in my humble opinion, *Robin and Marian* is the best movie ever, ever, ever made.

Think about it: Sean Connery as the aging Robin; Audrey Hepburn as the abbess Maid Marian; Nicol Williamson as Little John—the real one; Robert (oh, my God) Shaw as the moralistic and dashing Sheriff of Nottingham; not to mention Richard Lester directing and James Goldman's writing. It's enough to make a grown woman cry and always does. To be perfectly honest, sob is a more proper description.

"Swash my buckle," Nick promised, crossing his heart. "Come, my pretty, let me show you my etchings."

And he led me up the stairs and to a room three doors down from mine at the corner of the big old house. The room was enormous by SS standards. Windows on three sides (read that: cross-ventilation). The furniture did not match, but there was enough of it. Two armchairs next to a reading table, a double bed facing a decent-sized television and—stop my heart—a VCR.

"I'll get the Dixie cups, Nick. It's the least I can do."

"Uh, uh," he waggled his finger at me, "this hootch costs about a C-note a bottle. We will use tumblers, like civilized aristocracy. Unfortunately, there is only one, but I figure we swap enough spit on stage that it doesn't really matter."

At which point, I did what I would have sworn could not be done. I laughed and laughed, loud and real, and with such relief and genuine joy I might have suspected myself of having a multiple-personality disorder had I wanted to spoil the moment. So I just laughed some more and settled on the big (sagging) bed with my legs crossed while Nick presented me with a water glass full of cognac and then went to diddle his apparatus like a fifteen-year-old boy showing off for his friends.

Nick had not lied. *Robin and Marian* was all cued up and ready to go. He turned on the small reading light on the table and turned off the overhead as the credits began to roll.

"This is my favorite movie in the world," he said and took the glass from my hand. He sipped appreciatively and handed it back to me as we settled back into the pillows. I supposed that when you are a star, you get four pillows. I had yet to merit more than two.

"You really are a shit, Jacobs."

"Aw, you noticed. What gave me away?"

"You've got this wonderful, sensitive, humble, handsome crap down to a science." I sipped, too, and the brandy was the best I had ever tasted. "And let us not forget, funny, tasteful, generous . . ."

"Shall I mute the sound so I can hear you better?"

"No, you shit. The beginning in the Arab prison with crazy Richard [Harris] the Lionhearted is one of my favorite scenes. I'll just shut up instead."

"Well, if you insist," he said, taking the glass once again and placing it gently on the nightstand on my side.

And as he leaned over to position the cognac, he kissed me.

It was a slow, measured sort of kiss. I heard the glass make muffled contact with the paint-slopped wood of the end table and then felt his left hand move to cup my right cheek. His thumb stroked languid circles at my jawline as the kiss went on and on and on.

There was no urgency, just an overwhelming sweetness. The softness of his lips was sensual beyond any caress I had ever experienced. With excruciating deliberateness, he pulled my poutier lower lip between both of his and then released it, just to give equal attention to the upper.

That one kiss lasted all the way until Robin and Little John had made the entire journey back to England.

As Marian was preparing to be taken to jail by the Sheriff of Nottingham, the agonizingly exploratory butterfly touches swelled. Nick's hand wove itself into the soft, straighter hair at the back of my neck. He pulled his face three or four inches away from mine and searched my eyes for compliance.

He saw bucketloads of that. Our gaze was as locked as a cat on a sparrow, though even now I could not say which of us was which. All I know is that, never in my life have I *needed* a man before.

Oh, I've wanted them. Some, like Duchinski, quite desperately and for long periods of time; but never the way I wanted to touch every inch of Nick Jacobs.

This was Victoria Bowering's definitive "mad scene."

That is not an excuse, but no truly sane person could ever have felt the way I did at that moment. There was nothing else on earth: no near-lovers or ex-husbands, no alley cats or unemployment. I was lifted to a place where only touch existed.

And for the next two and a half hours. And for some time after the videotape had rewound itself.

After two years of being pushed away when I was most vulnerable—admittedly for all the higher moral reasons—it was like a miracle that I should be pulled toward, when less vulnerable but ever-so-much-more alone.

And for the first time in recorded history, Victoria Bowering said nothing but "Oh, God," for an entire evening.

They were also the first words she uttered when she awoke in Nick Jacobs's bed an hour before dawn.

TEN

I KNOW WHAT you're thinking.

Yes, I do, because I was thinking the same thing: Vic, you slut, how *could* you?

Just as I rolled over and stretched that catlike stretch that women do before they are fully awake, I was sure that it was sometime in the 1980s. After all, there was a long, warm body next to mine. Running my foot up the expanse of leg and repositioning my arm to the center of the rhythmically rumbling chest, I encountered no resistance from nasty old pajamas.

Obviously, I thought, I had mysteriously roused before my husband, Barry. It was the most logical of explanations for a woman who had not spent the night with a man for, well, an unbelievably long period of time. After all, I had my principles.

And Bowering principle number one was, no sleeping with men. Sex was allowed under the benignest of situations, B.D. (Before Duchinski), but no sleeping *ever*. And for those of you who have been paying attention, it had been approximately three years, two months, and a week or two since there had even been the sex part without so much as a doze.

Bowering truth number two is that for one hour upon coming out of sleep, I am allowed to be as stupid as a bucket of hair. It will be so anyway, so why beat myself up over it? Right?

Well, you know those sudden explosions of realization that shoot your eyes so quickly and completely open that you're afraid you'll never get your eyelids lowered ever again? I thought so.

I had one of those.

Big time.

First, Barry did not snore, no matter how melodically. He prided himself on it, though I thought it showed a certain shallowness of nature. Ergo, to wit, my bedmate was not Barry Laskin.

Second, Dan Duchinski might comfort me through some traumatic murder-type incident under great protest, but would swallow the barrel of his .38 police revolver before getting naked with me. This has been documented on occasions too numerous to list in such a short narration.

Without moving another muscle, I swung my sight at a truly painful acute angle to the right. Through the poorly crocheted veil of red hair, I could make out one well-trimmed ginger mustache and matching stubble—sprinkled evenly like jimmies on a vanilla ice-cream cone.

I disengaged myself as carefully as a bomb squad veteran, unable to prevent an exhalation of my new mantra.

"Oh, my God."

Nick whiffled on, oblivious, and replaced my body with a spare pillow.

Somehow, I had to find my clothes (or at least most of them), dress (at least mostly), and sneak down the hall back to my own room before any one of the twenty-two other people hanging around like the inhabitants of a giant roach motel caught me en flagrante. I was not particularly worried about waking Nick.

After the prior evening's recreation, I figured he would be sleeping like the, pardon me under the circumstances, dead until an hour before the matinee. After all, he was even older than I, and I was/am unashamedly thirty-ninish.

By some miracle, I located all my strewn clothing and got them over my body, right side out. With a grimace, I painstakingly opened the door to the hall just wide enough for me to squeeze through.

Because I was still in my bucket-of-hair state, I was unnaturally relieved to note that no one was wandering the house at five-fifteen A.M. and sprinted into my cubicle, shutting the door quickly, with my heart beating as though I had just made off with the crown jewels.

Which, in a way, I guess I had.

Shame and guilt smacked me up the side of my head, closely followed by a tremor of—and no one could have been more shocked than I—ravenous desire.

Cleopatra, Queen of Denial, wanted nothing more at that moment to jump back into those rumpled sheets. I reasoned, in that way I do, that the harm was already done and so . . .

I decided to take a shower. It would probably be the last time before the show that it would be empty anyway, let alone give up hot water.

My luggage was still packed, so I dug around for clean underwear and an XXXL T-shirt and made directly for the bathroom six feet down the hall from my room.

The water pressure was blessedly blasting and I decided to

take Khaki up on her offer of conditioner. And soap. And shampoo. Khaki would want me to be clean and my stuff was still crammed somewhere in the guts of my suitcases.

Not that I really believed I'd ever be clean again. Damn my New England upbringing. Soaping up excessively, I could not stop thinking of Dan. Dan had his damnable ethics and scruples and all those other repulsive moral problems, but I (damn, damn, damn) loved him. I had for years now. Hell, *Slasher* loved him, and he loved Slasher, and how many heterosexual men are there in the world who could find it in their little hearts to love a damned *cat?*

And while the big old ethical cop was worrying about me down the road at a bed and breakfast, I was schtupping what few brains I had left out with some, some *television* actor.

I should be killed. No doubt about it, there was no punishment on earth horrendous enough to get me back for my slatternly behavior. Unethical. Immoral.

I grabbed Khaki's Nexxus shampoo, wondering what a detergent more expensive than my usual brand X would do to my recalcitrant curls.

It would serve me right if every red hair fell out and into the drain and I had to do the rest of the run wearing a heavy, ugly, hot polyester wig.

Yes, that would do it. And because I would be stark bald underneath the ugly wig, it would keep slipping off, and the hair would never grow back, or—yes, better—it would grow back *brown. Mousey* brown. Shampoo ran into my eyes and I was glad that it hurt as I scrubbed and scrubbed at my scalp. A cold breeze washed over my wet body and I was happy at how my skin bumped up in discomfort. Yes. Yes, a rash, too. Serves me right. Serves me damned right.

But God was having another slow day, punishing me by refusing to punish me, and soon I was enveloped again by gushes of warm steam.

And slow, accomplished hands massaged the back of my neck and my hair, taking the excess suds down my back and over my buttocks. I aimed my face into the stream of water to clear my eyes as the phantom hands roamed, lubricated by Khaki's self-indulgent hair-care product.

I still wonder what Dan would have done under the circumstances. I even wonder how Queen Elizabeth II would have reacted. Or not, as the case may be.

I turned around. Clever, huh?

Nick was slick with perspiration and shampoo, his mouth on mine and hands everywhere else as the stream of water slicked the Nexxus from my hair (which, incidentally, I still seemed to have).

"Oh, my God," I said, coming up for air.

"Nope," Nick answered. "Just little old me."

Well, I guess we all know that was a misstatement if ever there was one. And, okay, yes, despite my very best—and they were really good best-intentions—and the laws of nature and physics, two very tall, rather middle-aged actors made happy, raunchy, gee-I-like-you love standing up in a mildewy shower until the water ran cold and the cast house began to stir.

"Oh, my God."

I had actually managed to deteriorate mentally from a bucket of hair to a lump of sodden redundancy.

And it was good.

Nick nodded his head toward the bathroom door and the noises evolving from opening doors and enthusiastic yawns. How long had we been standing underwater? How long would it take to get the prune wrinkles off my entire body?

"My baby, God but you are exquisite when you're wet." He kissed the cup at the center of my neck. "Let's just stay here all afternoon." He kissed my jawline and right ear. "It would be noble. We could let our understudies be stars."

I heard the bathroom door open from behind the shower curtain.

"Oops," Khaki apologized. "Didn't think anyone else would be up. Khaki will wait, but could you hurry, because she really needs to use the potty, or can I just go ahead while you finish? By the way, who is in here?"

I stuck my finger into Nick's chest and nodded to him. If I said it was me, Khaki would just park herself on the Jane and wait to comment on the deterioration of my physical features since the night before. Nick seemed to understand.

"It's Nick, Khaki, I'll be right out."

"Oops, oops, oops."

Nick covered my mouth with his big hand to keep me from giggling. Not that I was going to, but it was not an unreasonable option.

"No problem, Khaki darlin', I'll be right out!" he said.

"Khaki will check downstairs, you just take your time, Nick. Sorry. Sorry."

The door clicked shut and we listened to Khaki's "oops, oops, oopses" all the way down the hall and the back stairs to the first floor.

"Oh, my God," I breathed and stepped out of the shower, grabbing for my pile of clothes. Of course, I had forgotten a towel, but you all know how I can get. So I slipped the XXXL tee over my wet body, sans underwear. Discretion being the better part of valor, I figured I would borrow another of the dead Garrett's towels when I was safely ensconced in the privacy of my own cell. Nick stood casually naked as a jaybird (oh, my God) watching my progress.

"NYPD, huh?"

I looked down at the crumpled tee stuck to the few curves I had. It was one of Dan's shirts.

"Uh-huh," I nodded on my way to escape.

"I was going to do one of those, but my agent couldn't work out the details."

"Smart agent," I mumbled, and fled.

I got to my room unseen, though, logically, it would not have mattered.

Even though it is almost never true, casts usually expect the leading lady and man to have a "thing" during production.

I suppose it was knowing that Dan and Barry were just down the road that filled me with all the guilty terror of an eleven-year-old sneaking a cigarette while her parents are downstairs.

Speaking of which . . .

"Vic. Vic. You have company downstairs!"

I stuck a cigarette in my mouth and swung open the door to the wardrobe, which I sincerely hoped still contained the neatly folded linens of my deceased predecessor.

"Oh, my God."

There are predecessors, and then there are *predecessors*. No doubt I had just taken over Garrett Heinrich's final role: Miss Mona, in her room, and her lover's bed. Oh, my God. I was *really* going to be punished for this one. When Vic Bowering falls off the morality wagon, she just rolls for miles.

"Coming!" I screamed down toward the stairs, praying it

was my sister, Lydia, come to listen to my confession so that, should I meet with one of those contagious accidents going around the theater, I could go to heaven.

Bless Garrett's heart, there were dozens of perfectly folded celadon green towels to match the washcloth I had ruined on Nick's nosebleed. Reaching without looking, a stack of the beach towels fell to the wardrobe floor.

Foolishly, I wondered if that were the sort of thing that would make Garrett spin in her grave. I promised her wandering spirit to put them back exactly as they had been when I got back from the matinee.

I stripped off the T-shirt and did a quick mop up. My hair was still soaked, so I fluffed it, scrunching it into something resembling a hairdo for when it dried, dressed in the next outfit on the top of the luggage heap and headed toward the first floor.

Thank heavens for stage makeup. It was all still on my face where I had left it the night before. Most of it, anyway. There was that accusatory rosy beard-burn on my chin, which I had decided to ignore and hoped every one else would be too well-bred to mention. Needless to say, I ran into Jonathan Resnick on the stairs.

"Good night, Vic? You're going to need some industrial-strength foundation to cover up your sins. Between that and the black eye, you really look like shit."

"Thanks Jon, I appreciate your concern."

"No trouble at all, Vic. Put out that cigarette before I make you eat it."

I would joust with Jonathan later; at that moment, I just wanted to see my baby sister, the smart, pretty one, so I ran down the rest of the stairs two at a time.

Khaki was still wandering around looking for a bathroom,

and the chorus was assembled in the kitchen trying to find someone with the advanced educational degree to make coffee out of empty beer cans and auto-digested lettuce.

Spinning myself around the corner into the communal room to meet my company involved more athleticism than I expected, so it was with some vigor that I ran smack into the immovable force that is Dan Duchinski.

"Don't say anything, Vic," Dan admonished me, "until I apologize for last night."

Oh, my God.

"Dan, I . . ."

"No, Vic. I was wrong. Barry was wrong too, but he's too much of a wimp to come over and say so. We bullied you when we should have been supporting your decision. We both know that this is your career and, even if it's not what we would choose for anyone that we give a shit about to do with her life, it is your choice.

"Now, you know as well as I do that there's something rotten here in Denmark, but this is not my territory and I have no business in the middle of it except that I love you," *Oh, my God,* "and have to at least warn you to watch your ass. Okay? Okay.

"Last, I have asked Buck Sawicki to look after you—I know how you hate that—but it's done. He's psychotic and likes his hash a little bit too much, but I would trust him with my life, and have. He knows about the booby-trapped shot in your gun last night, too, and will be doing the loads himself from now on." Aha. *That* was what Dan wasn't telling Barry at the bar.

"Okay," I agreed. "I'm sure the shot was an accident though. I've had them overloaded before. Mostly they just set little fires."

Dan nodded to let me know that he thought I was full of it, but was not going to argue with me anymore.

"So, how about joining me and Barry for some breakfast before we go away and leave you to do whatever the hell it is that you think you have to?"

"I thought you were Lydia," I muttered.

"Let's get some food into you, babe. You know how you are before you wake up."

So I let him lead me away.

"Are you allergic to your stage makeup?" Barry asked the minute he saw me. "Your face is a mess."

"Yes," I lied evenly.

One of the nicest things about Barry is that while he is ignoring the obvious, he provides those around him with logical alibis. I guess that's what makes him the high-priced lawyer he is today.

Moving right along, I said, "Thank you both for the flowers. They're lovely. Very thoughtful." Dan looked at me with his X-ray vision.

"You sent flowers?" Barry asked Dan. That snapped him out of his examination of my face.

"What? Cops don't have the class to send flowers? Yes, I sent flowers. Of course, I sent flowers. Slasher is sending flowers tomorrow."

"What kind?" Barry could not resist asking, even though it made him look as juvenile as I knew he was.

The dining room of the bed and breakfast was really lovely. Small, with just five tables. Fresh flowers picked from the owner's garden sprung from every corner of the room and the center of each table. The walls were papered with a classic paisley pattern in warm ecrus and burgundies. And, take heart all healthy persons in America, the nonsmoking police had posted their mark. In keeping with the decor, the sign was hand-worked cross-stitch, beautifully framed, requesting "Thank you so very much for not smoking!"

I don't know about you, but I really hate any signage with an exclamation point at the end that warns of anything less than a toxic waste dump or plague.

"I'm going outside with the bugs for a cigarette while you guys work this floral thing out," I said and rose from my reproduction captain's chair. Too late. The fabulously picturesque innkeeper arrived at that moment from the kitchen carrying a pot of steaming coffee and three glasses of freshly squeezed orange juice.

She reeked of tobacco, and I concentrated on hating her politically correct guts. So much so, that I started to consider whether or not I was premenstrual. My incipient sense of fair play raised its ugly head.

I was just in one hell of a guilt-ridden, rung-out, post-coital bad mood. The kind of mood that Duchinski can sniff off me as surely as I could smell the Marlboros on our hostess's gingham apron. And when I start the guilt-spiral, it takes on a life of its own, whereby my unconscious starts seeking out every other extraneous irresponsibility I have ever committed over the course of thirty-ninish years.

"Who's watching Slasher?" I asked Dan.

"Your favorite superintendent, Carlotta. She was making him her special, from-scratch Romanian stew stuff he likes so much. He's fine. I'll be home to pump his stomach before dark."

I nodded and stared at my orange juice as though it would speak to me.

Dan knew about Nick and me. Not only did he know, but the son of a bitch *understood*. I really hated him for that.

"Do you have any hydrocortisone cream for that rash?" Barry asked. If I did not know better I would have sworn it was on purpose. "There have been several cases of flesh-eating bacteria reported in the New York Metropolitan area in the last few days."

Dan and I ignored him while the innkeeper delivered our breakfasts.

"I don't eat pork," Barry added, handing the plate back to the woman. I intercepted it.

"But I do," I said, scraping the bacon off the plate onto mine and placing the pigless eggs back in front of Barry. "It's an allergy," I explained to our host with a smile.

Extra bacon. That would serve me right.

I'd get fat. I would get fat and have very, very high cholesterol, and when I died at a tragically young age (not that that is actually possible by now) everyone would be too racked with grief to speak ill of the dead.

We did not converse again for the remainder of breakfast. I helped Dan and Barry load the car and they drove me back to the cast house with an hour to spare before half-hour call. My double bacon sat like a bowling ball at the bottom of my stomach.

Neither one of my erstwhile men got out of the car when I got out. They were deservedly objectifying my existence.

What caught their attention was the fire.

ELEVEN

SMOKE FELL HEAVILY from the hayloft door at the crest of the barn eaves. Whatever was burning was in the wardrobe department: a tumble of hand-me-downs, bolts of upholstery material, dressmaker dummies, wigs, and boxes of stuff I would never choose to closely examine.

It did not look good for the matinee performance.

Early audience arrivals milled around in the mostly empty parking lot, checking out the brand-new Hempstead Beach fire truck. A volunteer paramedic van was parked catty-corner to the spiffy red truck, with two civic-minded locals leaning against it, smoking and chatting.

Dan bolted from the red Toyota, pulling his shield from his shirt pocket to flash his way into the building. Very impressive, but no one seemed inclined to argue with the steaming hulk of policedom in any event.

As he stormed into the barn theater, he almost ran over my baby sister, Lydia, who was exiting in her calm, controlled way.

"It's okay," she announced to the assembly. "Smoky, but

nothing really caught. Nothing but some smoldering."

Did I mention my sister is also captain of her village's volunteer fire department? No? Well, Lydia has never been a mere joiner. She is the Rommel of all she surveys. I cringe to consider the outcome of World War II had she been born and in a position of Axis power.

"Lydia!" I called.

She waved casually and sauntered in my direction, stopping briefly to update the paramedics who, of course, believed whatever it was that she had to tell them, got into the van and pulled away.

"Vic! I'm so glad you called," she said, hugging me. "What happened to your face?"

"Age?"

"You know," she scowled at me. Really, she should have been the older one. Mother always said so. As it is, we are close enough in age that we have a tendency to speak in a nearly indecipherable shorthand. It always drove Barry crazy.

Instead of conversing A, B, C . . . , we talked around subjects starting somewhere like J, R, Z.

"Yeah," I shrugged in that R to Z way, admitting I had walked into something again without actually having to admit it.

"Got a seat for me this afternoon? I don't have to pick up any of the kids for a few hours." Barry got out of the car and joined us. "Hi, Barry," she almost acknowledged him. "Come here often?"

They hated each other now, though that had not always been the case. Lydia took Barry's leaving me rather personally. I love my sister.

Barry rose above the bait. "There might not be a show this afternoon, Lyddy."

She smiled benevolently. I believe that is called passive-aggressive behavior. If the Bowering sisters are truly gifted at any one thing, it is this.

"No damage, Barry. The fans will blow most of the stink out in fifteen minutes." I knew she had it timed to the second. She times everything.

Duchinski appeared at the barn doors with Buck Sawicki. Both men were red-faced and growling at each other. I ignored that, too.

"I'll arrange a comp ticket for you with the producers. I'm only supposed to get two for each play, but, hey, I'm the star, right?" At which time, Nick Jacobs swaggered around the corner of the theater and into the parking lot. Lydia shot me a quick glance after catching sight of Nick, as he joined Dan and Buck for an update.

"Read it in the papers," Lydia said.

"What?" Barry asked, still bogged down in the A or B part of the situation. He was not being stupid, he just had not acclimated yet.

"Let's see what's going on," I said, leading the way toward the three men at the door. Dan and Buck were still growling, so I shouldered past them to the box office. Charlie and Susan were in the office with Rod Verenes.

"At least cancel the matinee, Charlie," Rod argued.

"We're sold out," Susan countered. "As long as the fire is definitely out, and there is no danger, we can't afford to lose the revenue."

"She's right," Charlie agreed.

"By gawd, you two have got to be the most stubborn people I've ever met," Rod snorted. Not wanting to miss a straight line, I interrupted.

"Charlie and Susan, this is my sister, Lydia. Lydia, Charlie and Susan. And the guy in the uniform is Chief Verenes."

"We've met," Lydia smiled. Of course they had. I turn my back for one second, and my sister has already made her own introductions. What, I ask you, is the point of being raised properly when your gun is constantly being jumped?

"And fuck you, *too,*" Buck's voice blasted over my contemplation. Dan came up behind all of us at the office door. Knowing they had not met, I gave manners another whack.

"Lydia, this is Dan Duchinski. Dan, Lydia." There. That'd show them.

"Well," Lydia shook Dan's hand, "so nice to meet you at last."

"Tell your sister to leave," he ordered, a little more out of control than I am used to seeing him. "There's something wrong here, and you know she always ends up in the middle."

Lydia nodded, understandingly. I smacked her arm really hard. I mean *really* hard, like when I was eleven and she was eight or nine and I could get away with it. She smacked me back.

"She'll be okay, Dan," Lydia answered as though there had been no domestic violence. "I'm here now, and you know how she gets." Rod Verenes took his shot.

"Duchinski's probably right. Sorry, Charlie. Someone is trying to shut you down. Maybe you should accommodate him until we figure out who it is."

"Of course," Barry interjected because he just cannot help being an attorney, "if you shut down, you'll probably never find out who the perpetrator is. That wouldn't be logical."

Thank you, Mr. Spock.

"That's right," Charlie agreed. "He's right. No one was hurt, after all."

"Except maybe Garrett Heinrich," Rod answered. "Ayuh. Some folk might argue that she hurt plenty."

Admittedly, Chief Verenes's observation threw a bit of a pawl on that debate. But only a bit.

"Can my sister get a seat for the matinee?" I asked. Rod Verenes and Dan Duchinski threw their hands in the air in unison and pushed back to the outside.

"Of course," Susan said. "She may have to sit in the light bridge with Buck if there aren't any cancellations, though."

"Even better!" said my adventurous baby sister. If I did not know better, I would think she was trying to prove that she could climb a ladder and spend two hours with a psycho without injuring herself just to spite me.

"Half-hour!" Mr. Mike screeched from inside the theater.

"Thank you!" I screeched back right into the stage manager's face. He had appeared to open the doors to the waiting public. "Mike, will you find my sister a seat or direct her to the light bridge?"

"I want the light bridge," Lydia insisted.

"Fine. Then the light bridge, Mike?" He nodded in his adorably comatose way and led Lydia inside. I ran to catch Dan and Barry getting back into Dan's car. I do not know why I felt compelled to apologize, but I was.

"Guys, look, I'm sorry. I know everything is a mess here, but I really do appreciate your coming all this way to see the show, and the flowers, and," (egad!) "your well-intentioned advice, but you know I have to finish the run. It's what I do."

"I know," Barry heaved a sigh. I do believe he was more

concerned about my being snitty with him than he was for the professional completion of a season. Nonetheless, I appreciated it.

Dan slumped in resignation and pulled my face through the driver's window. He kissed me roughly.

"You watch yourself, Vic. I mean it. And listen to Buck. That means you pay more attention to him than you do to me, okay?" I wanted another kiss. "Okay?"

"Okay," I agreed.

"Now break a damned leg and call me if *anything* else happens. Capice?"

"Capice. Drive safely," I added moronically and waved them off.

What a day, and it was still early. And there were still two shows to perform. And Jonathan Resnick to face. He bagged me by the stage door entrance.

"Bowering, were you smoking in the wardrobe room?" Jonathan blew a cloud of smoke into my face.

"No. Were you?"

"The truth, Vic. The fire started with a cigarette thrown into a laundry bag. *Into* the bag."

"I wasn't even here, Jon. I have no idea who could have done it. As far as I know, the only people who even smoke around here are you, me, and Nick—who is strictly a cigar man. Besides," I snarled, "I'm not smoking anymore, remember?"

"Yeah, yeah. And there is peace in the Mideast." He opened the stage door for me to enter. From behind I could hear him finish, "And it wasn't your brand."

The show was not nearly as bad as it should have been, given the condition of the cast. Tremendous whistles of appreciation could be heard regularly from the light bridge. Lydia knew how to do that two-fingers-between-the-lips whistle I could never master, and I was gratified by her enthusiasm. It did not reach the levels she could achieve for her son's softball games, but, hey, he was still in his formative years and I was about as formed as I was going to get.

Since we ran late, food was brought directly to the theater for the cast so that we did not have to get out of costume to get something to eat between shows. After my delightful breakfast, I wasn't hungry, so Lydia and I walked back to the cast house for a catch up visit.

I introduced Lydia to the indefatigable Khaki, who was scuttling a buffet from the kitchen from hell with the aid of three chorines and Mr. Mike. Susan had managed to pull something well-balanced out of her hat during the performance and looked as though she had been dragged through Bosnia to do it.

"I could have made lunch," Lydia commented as we passed the last bus tray of food making its way down the hill.

"You still can," I agreed as we entered the cool interior of the big, old farmhouse. Lydia opened the refrigerator door, sighed, and removed two beers.

"I shouldn't," I protested weakly. Lydia popped both cans and handed me one.

"Live a little," she advised. "So?"

"What?"

"When did it happen?"

"What?"

"You know."

I did.

"Last night." Lydia tried to look disapproving, but failed, bless her little heart. "Several times." She crooked the infamous

Bowering eyebrow at me. "And once in the shower."

"Really?" Finally, I had impressed her. "Standing up?" She knew the answer to that one. She'd been a science major in college. I was not about to respond to a rhetorical physics/geometry question. "Wow."

"Wow," I agreed and downed my beer. "I'd better take a shower. Come on upstairs with me and keep me company. When do you have to leave?"

"About the time you dry off," Lydia answered and, taking her beer with her, followed me up the stairs.

I planted Lyd in my room and started the shower.

"I know, it's a mess, but I haven't had time to unpack yet."

"I'll bet," Lydia said, picking a towel off the wardrobe floor and throwing it at me. "You hose down and I'll tidy." She started refolding the plush green towels. Truly, only God can make a sister. I ran to the bathroom and took the shortest shower in the history of personal hygiene.

Still damp, I sat on the side of the bed to rummage through my bags for a make-do outfit. Lydia had already put my clothes away, and I found myself sitting on a small pile of papers. They stuck to my wet butt when I stood. Peeling them off, I asked, "What are these?"

"You tell me," Lydia answered, throwing me exactly the clothes I would have chosen myself. "The late Miss Mona's clothes are still in the drawers, so I moved the ones out of the top one for you. The papers were in the pile of towels."

"And?"

"Read them yourself."

"They're contracts," I observed brilliantly. "Not mine."

"Noooo," Lydia coached. I took my cue and read on.

"They're for a movie called, oh jeez, *Angel Drawers*." As I pulled on clothing, I continued to peruse. "Oh, they're Garrett's. But, huh, old contracts." I looked to Lydia for some help.

When faced with discovering something for myself versus being filled in, I will always prefer the latter—especially when I am about to pull a tunic over my head.

"And?" Lydia was not about to be any help at all. It was akin to being told to look up a word in the dictionary when you don't know how to spell it, for your own good. I was beginning to think that motherhood had had a profoundly poor influence on my baby sister. I yanked the tunic over my hips and read on.

"And the producers are a company called, jeez, Sweet Cheeks Productions. Sounds singularly smarmy, doesn't it? And why," I looked over at Lydia, arms crossed complacently at her chest, "would Garrett want to carry these with her if they are what we think they are?" Lydia did not even bother to prompt me with another well-placed "And?" "Because," I finished, shooting right to the Z of the monologue, "her leading man was Nick Jacobs."

"Bingo!" Lydia triumphed, and looked at her watch. "Gotta go. The kidkins are waiting for Mummy, and the working girls are waiting for Miss Mona." Sure enough, we had timed everything to the minute. "Race you to the car!" Lyd shouted as she sprinted out the door and down the hall.

Proving that my life had not become a total bag of buffalo chips, I beat her by six seconds minimum. She promised she'd come back again the next day while the kids were off doing productive, upwardly mobile things.

As I slammed on a thick cover of stage makeup I reveled in my racing win and contemplated the prospect of Nick Jacobs in what might have been a skin flick. It seemed unlikely.

Both the win and the porn.

Never underestimate the number of buffalo chips that can be contained in one woman's karma.

The second show of that Sunday started mechanically, as they almost always do, but by the end of the first act, the chips started to hit the fan.

TWELVE

KHAKI WAS THE first to drop like a sack of garbage stage right.

Technically, *Khaki* did not drop, but she certainly dropped her lunch all over the backstage flooring, which caused a massive pileup of sliding chorus people ready to make their entrance.

The vomit reflex action did much of the rest.

Mr. Mike, the stage manager, who had already taken possession of a bucket for himself, had the unfortunate duty of locating several others to be situated here and there while coughing up his own guts.

Of course, the show went on.

But it went on with cast members unceremoniously exiting stage right, left, or wherever, to barf into whatever was handy and reenter wherever they could.

To say that it was disorienting for me would be putting it mildly. Secondary lines were spoken by whomever happened to be onstage at the proper moment. In fact, it was a triumph of live theater that the show began and actually ended with any continuity whatsoever.

Nick was looking a little green, but did not need to make use of any receptacle during the show despite the wafting odor of bile making its way throughout the fanned theater.

I felt just fine, thank you. As a matter of fact, I felt so fine that I was cruising through the performance wondering what was wrong with this picture. I had come to accept many years ago that if there is manure to be stepped in, my high heels will be the first to make contact. But I felt just *fine*.

The audience, as usual, wanted a few more looks at the famous Nick Jacobs and they were willing to applaud through extra curtain calls to have them, but by the end of the show it had become an impossibility.

Chorus members were laid about the green room like fungus on a forest floor.

The paramedics arrived as the final strains of the orchestra sounded—in oh, so many ways. The intestinal devastation was so great by that time, Charlie Mackin and I were recruited to drive the residual sufferers to the local emergency room. Having no sense of direction whatsoever, I followed Charlie.

The ER doctor was very cute. The fact that I was in a position to notice only reiterates my fine health. He had a lovely British accent and crackling blue eyes that, were he taller, I would have found fascinating.

"I'd say we have a case of food poisoning, here," Dr. Hastings commented to Charlie and me.

"I'd say so," I said, kicking off my heels on the off chance that he would appear taller to me in my bare feet.

He did not.

"What common food did these people eat prior to becoming incapacitated?" The sound of retching from all corners of the ER detracted from the melodiousness of his deep bass voice.

"The commonest," I responded as Charlie held Jonathan's head over a bedpan. "There was a cast meal served between shows. Everyone had pretty much the same thing." Nick was hanging on to an institutional green wall for all his life, but still had not erupted.

"Potato or egg salad?" the doctor asked.

Charlie shook his head.

"No," I answered. "As far as I remember no mayonnaise food. Cold cuts, bread, pickles, fruit Jell-O I think."

Jonathan nodded.

"Odd," the doctor observed. "Did you eat with the cast?"

"Nope," I answered with gratitude to whatever. "My sister was visiting, so we just had a beer at the cast house." Jonathan threw me a venomous glare, but then reemptied himself before he could reprimand me.

"You?" he asked Charlie.

"I was taking a nap. I didn't have anything to eat at all before the show." He took a fresh bedpan from an overworked nurse. "Lucky for me, I guess."

"What about him?" Dr. Hastings gestured to the chartreuse Nick at the entrance to the holding room.

I looked to Jonathan, who was very busy with his own problems, and then to Charlie.

"He ate," Charlie said. "I remember Susan telling me that he was very happy to have red Jell-O for dessert. She commented on what a regular guy he is."

"Did you eat lunch with the cast, Nick?" I called to him. He could only manage a nod. More would have put him over the edge, I'm sure.

"Well, then," the doctor said with satisfaction, "looks as though we ought to get down to pumping a few stomachs, eh?"

Jonathan spewed, spit, and asked, "Will they be able to rehearse tomorrow?"

"Certainly," Dr. Hastings answered without hesitation, "but the stomach tube will probably give them some vocal problems—esophagal irritation, you know—for a few days. Will you all be able to work around that for a week or so?"

Jonathan and Charlie groaned together.

"No problem for me," I said gallantly. The doctor smiled adorably at me. I guess a woman who is the only one not drenched in semidigested food and bile is especially attractive at nine o'clock in the evening. "Nasty luck, we're doing a musical."

"Oops," Dr. Hastings said. "Then we had better do some laboratory testing on the good chance that we're going to have to prescribe some prednisone for the old vocal cords, eh? Wouldn't want to knock off the survivors, would we?" He chuckled in a very medical sort of way.

I chuckled back, but, then, I wasn't sick. Nick slumped into a green, plastic molded chair looking for all the world as though he were a piece of it.

"I'd say so," I said, lapsing without thought into the British physician's vocal meter.

Charlie took Jonathan to the rear of the room to lie down.

"I get off at ten," Dr. Hastings said. "I don't suppose you'd care to get a bite to eat? It seems you haven't had dinner yet."

Gotta love the Brits.

"Thanks, Doctor Hastings, but I think I'm going to be needed to drive this crew back home. Someone is going to have to hold their heads over the toilets for a few hours, don't you think?"

"I'm afraid so," he agreed. "Perhaps another time?"

"One can hope," I smiled, not really interested, but caught irretrievably in the flirt zone. I have gotten far too old to spend any more of the best years of my life in flats, so flirting was as far as that illicit relationship would go.

Another hour saw the final stomach pumped and the cast loaded into cars to get back to the cast house.

Nick still had not technically emptied his stomach on his own volition, but Dr. Hastings insisted it be done mechanically.

I—and probably Charlie—drove back toward the theater with the windows wide open.

Damn the coiffeur and full speed ahead.

Dan has always said that my fundamental shallowness would get me into trouble one day.

I just hate it when he's right.

So how could I resist making a call to let him know how very much all right I was? Besides, it would reassure me to hear Slasher's muffled snore over the phone.

My own answering machine voice answered the New York number, and I wished that Lydia were around to remind me how to change the message via the phone line. One look at the old rotary dial reminded me that it would not be possible anyway, so I left a meandering message.

You know the kind: stilted, jabbering, fraught with guilt, fear, and transparent optimism.

My specialty.

THIRTEEN

LYDIA ARRIVED, BRIGHT as a robin, at nine o'clock in the morning. Obviously, she has never held a position in the acting field, desolate as it may be. Nine A.M. does not even exist for those of us with union cards. Even so, there was no one else in the house capable of answering the door—like it was locked—and I figured subliminally that it had to be her.

Knowing me, as she does, she was carrying a thermos of black coffee and two Croissanwiches—sausage.

"Anyplace to eat?" she asked. "Besides the kitchen, of course."

"There's a living room around here somewhere," I answered. "I haven't . . ."

"I guess we *know* you haven't gotten there yet." With unerring accuracy she headed in the direction I believed to be the community TV room. Sure enough, she was right. It was not much cleaner than the kitchen, but there were some bare spots on furniture upon which she could balance the bag of food as she swept the foot-high pile of newspapers and tabloids off the coffee table.

Though the room was devoid of people, "Regis and Kathie Lee" was blaring from the old maple television console, as though it had simply landed catty-corner near the door direct from its trip through outer space. The vertical hold was not holding and Kathie Lee smiled broadly at a bizarre diagonal. On the other hand, I am no expert on how she looks at any time. I turned down the sound.

"Why don't you turn it off?" Lydia asked.

"Because cast house televisions don't usually turn back on," I said and parked myself on the colonial-style sofa with several telephone books propping up the corner without a leg.

The bookshelves were shoved haphazardly with show business auto- and biographies, a *Backstage* casting paper from two seasons before, several dog-eared scripts of classic plays no one working at this particular theater would ever perform, and empty Evian bottles.

Dancers love paying big money for water. Don't ask me why. I just report the news.

Lydia noticed the bottles as well.

"There's a free county spring right down the road," she said, handing me my faux breakfast and pulling a clean coffee mug out of her canvas shopping bag.

"I'll post a notice on the bulletin board." Actually, I would not bother, but Lydia knew that. She was just being organized, hoping without any faith whatsoever that I would follow.

"I read about the food poisoning," Lydia commented, pulling a *Portland Press Herald* from deeper in the recesses of her magic bag and tossing it to me.

"I never read before noon." I pushed the paper aside. "Eat,

and tell me about the kids. How's whats-his-name?"

"I try not to eat junk, and Richard is just fine. Last night he delivered twins." (Yes, we Bowering girls try to make at least one of our marriages to a professional. One apiece, that is.) "The kids are off at their sailing lesson."

"A Dick idea?" I chewed happily. Lydia scrunched up her mouth, trying to decide whether or not to defend her husband. She moved along, instead.

"What caused it?" She meant the vomit-fest from the night before.

"Food poisoning, I guess."

"Hard to believe the cast hadn't built up an immunity." She pulled a jockstrap from beneath one of the sofa cushions.

"Isn't it?" I tossed a still-damp leotard at her head.

"Vic, Vic, Vic," Lydia slowly shook her head side to side. "Vic," she added for extra pathos.

"I love you, too."

"So," the jump was approximately F to M, "what do you want to do this morning?" I was still chewing, so she went the extra yard from M to Q. "I have a phone card to call those porn producers and the car to get us to the hospital."

"Good woman." I stood. "Give me five minutes."

Lydia knew I meant fifteen and had the living room sanitized by the time I reappeared. I knew she would and did not comment.

I hate to encourage that sort of deviant behavior.

On the way to the hospital, we caught up with each other in our own sisterly/witchy fashion.

"So?" Lydia asked, meaning how much did I enjoy or not my liaison with Nick Jacobs.

"Uh, huh," I answered, meaning it was the top of Magic Mountain for me.

"Yeah?" Translation: so are you going back for more?

"Probably," I answered, which speaks for itself.

"And?" Lydia was really asking what the poop was with Barry and me, and who the hell is Dan Duchinski.

"It's complicated," I answered without a prayer of getting off that easy. "Could you speed up a little? I could get out and run alongside and make better time."

"One more point," she said, speeding up five miles per hour and still five miles under the speed limit.

"You're kidding." I commented on the uncharacteristic proximity of violations on Lydia's driver's license to her losing it. I admit it. It pleased me. Maybe the second crop of apples does not fall all that far from the first droppings.

"Dump Barry. Duch-whats-his-name is in love with you."

"It's complicated."

"I heard that," she pulled into the regional hospital parking lot. "It always is." She put the car into first gear and shut off the ignition. No automatic transmission for *my* sister. "Listen, Vic," (uh-oh) "you're not getting any younger."

"No, Lyd, *you're* not getting any younger. I, had you not noticed, am still younger than springtime."

"You know what I'm saying," she threw the car keys into her voluminous sack and got out, slamming the door overmuch, if you ask me.

"I know what you're saying," I followed her, as submissively as is possible for me, into the chintz-upholstered lobby.

"You find a doctor for the ER, and I'll call directory assistance. Who has jurisdiction?"

"That's Dick-talk," I chided.

"Touché. Who handles contracts for films? Which union?"

"Usually the Screen Actors Guild, but I don't know if there is a separate porn guild."

"Is there a local in Boston?"

"I have no idea. Professionally, I can't seem to get arrested in any local performing union."

"We all pray that that is true, Vic. Especially Mother."

"Oh, go *phone,* and stop nagging me."

I followed the red arrows that indicated the direction of the emergency room from the main lobby, got lost only twice, and finally ended up trailing the sound of Rod Verenes's distinctive voice.

"Chemical?" Rod asked the doctor on duty.

"Absolutely," answered the East Indian woman. "Botulism would have killed at least one of the victims. Certainly most of them would have required hospitalization and none did. Salmonella bacterium is easily seen on a slide and there was none."

"Any idea'h what kind of chemical?" Rod asked. My eavesdropping gifts were obviously improving. I did not think Verenes knew I was standing nearby. Of course, I am also the woman who thought marriage was forever, and still sort of do.

"I will need confirmation from the state lab, but I am rather certain the victims ingested large quantities of propranolol," the doctor stated firmly enough that *I* sure believed her.

"Of *course!*" the talentless eavesdropper in me blurted.

"Why 'of course'?" Rod asked me. "What is this proprano stuff, Doctor?"

"It's a very common beta-blocker. Often prescribed for angina. Doctor Hastings suspected beta-blockers when he observed consistently low blood pressure among all the patients. Propranolol is the generic term."

Rod Verenes turned his steely gaze upon poor little me, then shot another question to the doctor.

"How so?"

"Well," the woman continued evenly as though it were the most obvious answer on the planet, "Doctor Hastings did some acting while at university in the U.K."

"Which, I believe," Rod again turned in my direction, "might be furth'ah explained by our actress he'ah?"

My gut reaction was to play dumb, but the way Rod Verenes was examining me, I knew it was too late to take the easy way out. I only use the stupid ploy when dealing with people so much more stupid than I am that there is an off chance they will buy it.

Sigh.

"Propranolol is also commonly prescribed for stage fright. The drug reduces anxiety without sedating." I shrugged.

Why not? I was innocent on this baby. Without my artistic anxiety, I stink up the whole stage.

"Is this true, Doctor?"

"Quite true, Chief Verenes. Many medical students take a small dosage before rounds to reduce their chances of freezing up upon professorial query."

Wow. I love talk like that.

"Wow," Rod echoed my thoughts, though for completely different reasons. I just did not know *which* completely different reasons. "You have medical training, Ms. Bowering?"

"Nah, I was a science major in college and I find it interesting, that's all."

That's all. Sure, that's all. That's *never* all when one is dancing the Vic Bowering masochistic tango. (Apologies to Tom Lehrer.)

Personally, I think I am about the most innocuous person walking around the face of the earth. I will never understand why the minute—the second—the word *victim* is used in a sentence, wary eyes are cast in my direction. Those of you who have been paying attention to my life know this is not the first time I have gotten one of those "hmmmmmm" looks from an officer of the law. And I don't mean "Hmmmmm, nice legs," either.

"Mind my askin' why you're here?" he asked, entirely too politely for my taste.

When in doubt and the truth doesn't seem to be working, lie, that's my motto.

"Jonathan wanted to know when it would be okay to start up rehearsal again for the new show." That sounded good. "It's an original and will need much more time than an old show. You know, no one has ever heard the music . . ." Stop me before I kill again. ". . . so we have to go over it a lot more than if we have recordings or stuff, or saw the show on Broadway or something . . ." *Help!* ". . . you know." I ended with a whimper rather than the more preferable bang.

"Vic, you ready to go?" my sister saved my butt, sort of.

Lydia has one of those faces that gets her elected chairperson of everything from the DAR to the IRA. Her appearance in any room will automatically diffuse any situation. If the government would send her to Beirut or Jedda or one of those other fun spots, there would be instant peace. And so it happened in that tiny emergency room in the middle of nowhere.

I can't explain it. We share the same parents and the same childhood environment.

Mother denies any responsibility, but I've seen our birth certificates.

Mother also advised Lydia and me to never ever tell a lie, because our noses would grow and God would punish us. Perhaps I should pay more attention to Mother.

Charlie and Susan Mackin led the entire *Whorehouse* cast into the emergency room.

Oops.

Jonathan took over, as directors do.

"We're going to need some steroids here," he rasped. "The cast sounds like the Vienna Dock Workers Choir—even Khaki, who can usually shatter lightbulbs with her upper register." Khaki nodded miserably, tears slopping down her cheeks. "What did that doctor use last night to pump our stomachs, a garden hose?" Jonathan sounded like Jack Klugman after his throat surgery. It was not pretty.

"I will need to examine all of you before I can prescribe anything to give you relief," the doctor advised. "Please line up in an orderly fashion and I will take you all as quickly as possible."

"Me first," Jon grumbled, "I have some yelling to do." He led the doctor behind the examination curtain.

Susan Mackin leaned against a wall and closed her eyes.

Lydia nudged me. "She looks awful. Maybe I should get the doctor to take her next."

"She didn't eat with the cast. She's just wrung out." Lydia crooked the questioning eyebrow. "It's been a rough season in the SS. I'll explain it all later."

Khaki started to sob. She rasped, gurgled and hiccupped. Her shoulders shook as though we were caught in an earthquake. Little Jon put a reflexive arm around her back to let her cry it out, but she bolted and ran into my arms.

Her voice was reduced to a baritone whisper.

"Vic, oh, Vic," she wept. "Khaki's beautiful lyric soprano voice is *ruined*. What is she going to do?"

Lydia's eyebrow shot all the way to her hairline.

"You're going to be fine, Khaki," I reassured her pathetically. Lydia, disappointed once again with my absolute dearth of nurturing skills, took Khaki from my arms and held her securely, stroking her baby-fine blond tresses and cooing. Little Jon, sensing a real talent in the "Mother will make it all better" department, joined us. He was sounding a lot like Walter Matthau, which is not bad, unless you're a twenty-something pretty-boy.

"We're quitting," Little Jon announced. Susan, overhearing, folded her arms around herself and dropped her head wearily. "This is," he had a coughing attack and continued, *"nuts."* More coughing until he gagged himself. Lydia rubbed his back, the way that mothers do. Khaki reattached herself to me and croaked.

"It's too dangerous, Vic. Khaki has her whole *career* ahead of her. She just can't do it anymore." She looked very determined, especially for Khaki. "We aren't safe here."

Susan planted Charlie in a seat next to the silent Nick Jacobs. Charlie looked the worst of all of us. His color had gone from pasty to a light powder blue. I was happy that we were already in a hospital; it would not have surprised me if it was Charlie who ended up admitted. Rod Verenes stood before the couple, discounting Nick for the moment.

"They're right, you know," Rod said. "This is way outta hand. It's a miracle that no one else has died."

"What do you mean?" Charlie asked.

"Buck Sawicki and the Smokeys did a thorough examination of the wiring in Garrett Heinrich's dressing room." He looked over at me and my growth, Khaki. "There was tampering. It was expertly done, but it was done, Charlie."

"The State Police confirmed that?" Susan asked. She had turned the same ghastly beige as the tiles on the floor and grasped onto her husband even more tightly than before. I saw her slip a tiny white pill into her husband's hand.

The cast line was moving along slowly. Jonathan came around the curtain clutching a small brown bottle of pills.

"So Garrett was murdered," Nick commented blandly.

"Seems so," Verenes confirmed, watching Nick closely.

Nick shook his head in disbelief and harrumphed an indecipherable noise. A dimple appeared in his left cheek.

"The tabloids," Nick cleared his throat and went on, "are going to have a field day with this one."

Susan's face was a mask.

"They already are," she said. "There are about forty messages for you at the office. I'm just leaving the machine on. You can listen to them at the theater whenever you feel like you can deal with them. About half are from your agent." Nick threw his head back. He had not shaven, and his Adam's apple stuck out like a forested mountain in his throat. If it would not hurt, I think he would have laughed.

And if it were a physical possibility, I believe Lydia's eyebrow would have airlifted itself right off her forehead.

Little Jon marched himself over to Chief Verenes and whispered hoarsely but loud enough to be heard for several feet.

"Jonathan couldn't *pay* for that kind of publicity for his stupid, piece of shit musical of his." Jonathan lurched directly to Little Jon's face, beet red, fists clenched.

Susan stood between the two of them.

"Now you listen to me, you two narcissistic dirtbags." That caught everyone's attention. "Charlie and I are on the verge of losing everything we have spent the last thirty years building, there are twenty very, very sick people here, one woman dead, and you two are having a *lover's quarrel?*" Charlie's quiet statement interrupted Susan.

"All my plans. All of them. Gone."

Susan darted back to her husband immediately, leaving the big and little Jons blustering in silence. Big Jon at least had the good manners to look a little ashamed. Just a little, though.

Susan soothed Charlie, murmuring a litany of the wonderful things that no one could take away from them: their children, their marriage, their future together. For some reason, it made me feel much worse. I don't know how Charlie was doing, except that his face was now a sheen of cold sweat, cut with lines of tears. Nick continued to stare at the acoustical tile ceiling, breathing rhythmically.

"Exit, stage left," I mumbled to Lydia. Another sufferer came out from behind curtain number one with a bottle of drugs. I was wanting outside and a cigarette very badly, indeed. Nick grabbed my hand as I squeezed past toward the door.

"See you back at the ranch, Dale?"

"It's a date, Roy."

He rubbed the top of my hand in his and laid his head back against the cool wall with a small smile.

The air outside was heating up, burning off the morning dew and mist. I knew my hair was doing its geriatric Shirley Temple thing. Lydia used to iron it for me, way back when Twiggy was making my life a nightmare.

"Okay, so you're not going to hell when you die," Lydia said from behind me. That meant that, in my position, she probably would have boffed Nick Jacobs, too. More efficiently, no doubt, but it would have been done.

"Thank you, Mother Teresa."

"You're welcome," she said, getting into the passenger side of the car. "You drive. I want to start making a list."

Here we go again.

My sister and I inherited this dread "listus vulgaris ad nauseumus" disease from our presumed mutual mother. Under duress of any kind—and I mean *any* kind—we make lists. They are always very *neat* lists, in our very *best* printing.

We write things down that we are worried about, should worry about, or will worry about when the schedule permits it. We also make lists of things we've already done, so that we can have the satisfaction of crossing them off the list.

After a lot of thought, and really a minimum of therapy, I have come to terms with this affliction as a non-life-threatening neurosis, sort of like nail-biting, but less cosmetically deleterious. It is just that it is so much *worse* when my family is together.

I got behind the wheel as Lydia pulled a notepad, pen, and car keys from her purse.

"Push down, to the right and back," she muttered, instructing me on the position of reverse—like I didn't *know*.

"You know," I said, informing her psychically that I had no intention of keeping to the speed limit.

"I know you've never gotten a ticket in your life. Someday you're going to have to walk me through your technique." She started writing. "I've been *with* you at least ten times when you've been pulled over. I just can't see your face when you accede to the fuzz."

"It's a gift," I said, roaring off on the country road back toward the cast house.

"When was the last time you drove standard?" she asked.

"Two, three years ago. It's like riding a bike," I answered, double-clutching down into second gear for an especially terrifying curve.

"More like seven years." She scribbled something onto her notepad and pondered another second before resuming. "You don't have to double-clutch to downshift anymore, and if you drop my transmission, I'll have to tell Richard I did it to save your life."

"You can tell Dick . . ."

"You tell him."

"Oooo, oooo," I noticed the tape deck.

"Watch your driving."

"A Samuel Ramey tape." I held it up, admiring the title cover and Ramey's chest hair. He was dressed as Attila. All right, so it is only exciting to me. "Can I?"

"You *may.*"

"Thanks, Lyd." I slid the tape in and cranked the volume up so high that the dashboard rattled as Samuel Ramey blasted out the bottom of his register. Lydia let me to my idiocy because she loves me and because by then she was completely immersed in her list.

The list was done by the time I wheeled in a cloud of dust and gravel up to the door of the cast house.

Preoccupied but ever-functional, Lydia popped the trunk of her car while I listened to the final soaring notes of the fabulous bass/baritone and pulled out an ice chest full of beer. She positioned it on the front porch, settled onto the glider, pulled out her Swiss Army knife from the bottomless bag of tricks, and opened two bottles. Handing me one, she started to read.

"I have here a list of suspects." She flipped the page. "Here, I have a list of motives. You'll have to fill me in on opportunity and anything I might have forgotten or missed. By the way."

She pulled out her calling card and tore another piece of paper from the back of the pad. "This is the number of the Screen Actors Guild. They wouldn't give me any information because I'm not a member and I couldn't remember your social security number."

"I don't suppose you . . ."

"Sweet Cheeks Production Company, Los Angeles, California. Nineteen eighty-two."

"Thanks."

I called, but had to dig my social security number out of my wallet before SAG would tell me anything. Of course, if I ever worked enough weeks to be eligible for unemployment compensation, I would have my number memorized. I guess that says it all.

The official voice on the other end of the line referred me to a list of Unfair Producers and backlogged to 1982.

"They're listed," he said. "And for two years prior to eighty-two. Pretty good. They were never signatories with the union."

"What kind of unfair stuff were they producing?" I asked.

"We don't list that," he answered in a way that made me understand that even though he was working a shit, uncreative job at a desk, that he had the inside dope because, if he had ever had a break, he would be a star.

"C'mon," I urged, "you guys know everything."

"Well, Sweet Cheeks went out of business in 1983." He wanted some more kissing up. I had some left in me, so what the hell.

"You *do* know. I can hear it in your voice. You're an actor, aren't you?"

"Well," I could almost hear him stifling a humble smile, "I used to be."

"AFTRA, too, right?" How long was this going to take?

"Yeah, I did some voice-overs."

"I *knew* it." I decided to cut to the chase. This was, after all, long distance. "But not for Sweet Cheeks Productions, I'll bet."

Suddenly, from across the phone line came a series of gasps, groans, and grunts. I was reminded of a movie, but I couldn't remember which one.

The voice returned in words, rather than animal noises. "But I *could* have, you understand?"

When Harry Met Sally! The fake orgasm scene!

"Thanks. You are really wonderful. Thank you so much."

"Hey, that's what I get paid for."

"Bye-bye."

"Bye-bye."

I was exhausted. The personal charm thing is much easier face-to-face. Or, as Lyddy pointed out, face-to-cop face.

So Garrett Heinrich and Nick Jacobs had done a little professional bumping of uglies before Nick made his breakthrough. Interesting. I don't usually get freebies.

"Okay, so you were right," I admitted to my sister.

"Thought so," she said and made an entry onto the motive page.

"But they were lovers."

"Who said that?"

Hmmmm. I could not remember. Maybe no one said it. Maybe it was that old leading lady/leading man assumption at work.

"I know I heard that it was a condition of Nick's contract

that Garrett come along as his co-star. But . . ."

". . . if they weren't lovers, why would he insist on that?" Lydia finished for me. We were beginning to do our two people–one sentence bit. Very efficient. Along with the alphabet topic-jumping, I am sure that, after a week or two together, we would not have to speak at all. We would be like a bus-and-truck of a bad *Star Trek* episode.

"That would explain why he didn't seem terribly . . ." I wanted to say devastated, but it wasn't necessary.

". . . and why Garrett would have those contracts squirreled away in her things." Lydia nodded with satisfaction.

"Blackmail." It was not a question. I thought for a moment, shutting down any residual good sense pushing at my brain stem. "It doesn't make sense. If Nick wanted Garrett out of the way, why all the other accidents? As he said, the tabloids . . ."

". . . will have a field day with this one." Lydia looked at me patiently.

"Publicity." The word felt dirty in my mouth. My mouth felt dirty, along with a few other places.

"Garrett is the only person who has actually died. Maybe Nick doesn't want to waste any more time out here in the hinterlands when he has already accomplished what he set out to do. Kill Garrett, get a stage credit, and pile up some headlines." Lydia polished off her beer, waited for me to finish mine, and opened two more.

I sucked mine down in silence. Lydia reached into her canvas bag and pulled out a hip flask. We have matching ones for when Dad takes us ice fishing. I will explain all such extraneous oddities of my upbringing at a later time. She offered it to me.

"Right," I swigged. Cognac. We always filled our flasks

with cognac and told Dad it was bourbon so he would not think we were being girly. I, naturally, had come to love bourbon. "There won't be any rehearsal today. Not by the looks of my peer group."

"Don't be silly." Lydia tried to lighten the mood. "You're too tall to have a peer group. That's the reason you were never able to get work in the chorus." She toasted me, feeling (I think) bad about planting seeds of doubt in my extramarital bed.

Aha! I lit a cigarette and sucked the smoke right down to my pedicure.

"But Nick was poisoned, too." There. I felt better.

"And yet, miraculously, not nearly as sick as everyone else. You told me yourself that he didn't even hurl."

"He was sick. You saw him yourself today. I'm sorry to report, he just isn't that good an actor."

"I'm sure." She took a gulp of cognac and waited for me to catch up again.

"So he underdosed himself."

"Bingo!" Lydia turned back to the suspect page of her notes. "Still, we have Little Jon . . ."

"Who would do almost anything to scuttle Jonathan's chances of success right about now."

"And the squeakster, Khaki, always the bridesmaid . . ."

". . . and never the leading lady. That's true. I don't know if you noticed, but . . ."

"That third-person routine. Yeah, yeah. And what about the psycho I sat with to watch the show. Mr. Tattoo."

Hmmmm.

"Dan told me to trust him. They know each other," I defended either Buck or Dan, I do not know which.

"I'll bet," Lydia observed. "He regaled me—in quite

colorful language—with the tale of how the producers would not sign off with the parole board to allow him to leave the state to set up their new theaters. He was, may I say, annoyed?"

"You may. I didn't know that. But, the way things are, those new theaters aren't much more than a pipe dream."

"Speaking of which," Lydia started packing up her duffle, "the cast is back and I have high moral standards to inflict on my children."

"Since they're not going to pick any up from their dear Auntie Vic."

"Bingo!" Lydia stood up as the caravan of cars pulled up behind her's.

"Don't forget your cooler," I reminded her.

"Opening night gift," she said and gave me a hug. "Love you."

"Love you more," I said, waving her off.

"Oh," she stopped at the bottom of the steps, "do me and your other heirs a favor and sleep with your eyes open."

I gave my sister my older sibling exasperated look and waved her away. Sure. Like I was going to crawl into bed with Nick Jacobs again.

Oh, sure.

Like he was even up to it.

Oh, sure.

Like he could possibly know how I "get."

Oh, sure.

Damn. He already did.

And, speaking of which again, why hadn't Dan called back? Or did I already know the answer to that one, too?

I opened another beer on the rail of the porch and waited for the cast to hobble into the house. Nick was out of the van first, shot me a huge smile, and helped the weaker folk out of the cars. I couldn't help myself and smiled back. God, but is that man handsome.

Jonathan was next to me first. Long legs, I guess. He looked like shit.

"No rehearsal today, Bowering, and put out the fucking cigarette." Oh, yeah, like I could sound worse than anyone else on that sunny, hot Monday. He handed me a bag full of cans of Campbell's chicken broth. "You're cooking dinner." He took a drag off my cigarette, turned ashen, and opened the screen door. "Fucking pride of Teutonic womanhood." The door slammed.

Nick got the last of the walking wounded up the steps and into the cool house before falling next to me on the glider.

"Alms for the poor?" he asked, pointing at the cooler.

"I thought you guys were all on broth and gruel for the day." Human color had returned to Nick's drop-dead (pardon me) gorgeous face.

Why me? After a dry spell that lasted almost three years, why do I have to go to the bother of flipping over enough rocks to come up with a sex partner who was probably a cold-blooded murderer?

It wasn't that I was desperate. There were hundreds of completely unsuitable men who approached me for meaningless, shallow sex every week in New York.

"Trigger is feeling much better," Nick said. He reached into the ice and pulled out two more frosties. Letting out a sigh, he unscrewed both caps. I started to laugh in that lovably raucous way I have about me. "What's so funny, Dale? Not me, I hope."

"Nope." I think I laughed so hard that mucus blew out my nose. I delicately checked with my forearm and finished, "I'm laughing at my sister and me." He waited patiently for an explanation as he sipped slowly at his beer. "We've been using an opener!"

He did not get it.

What I was saying was, that despite the lists, the high IQs, the damage done to our little psyches during adolescence and requisite lessons learned, my sister and I had been wrong. Together.

"You know what would make me a very happy camper?" Nick asked after finishing his beer. "Come to bed and just hold me while I take a nap." He appeared abashed at the request.

I *hate* it when men appear abashed. It is my very, very least favorite expression of discomfort to be spread over a man's face. First of all, I don't believe it, and second of all, men are not supposed to be vulnerable. It is written down in *all* the books—particularly those read by men.

Well, okay, no one is more vulnerable than an ill man, but they aren't supposed to *show* it. And psychopaths looking vulnerable are just too incongruous, too manipulative, too . . .

"I promise I won't compromise you, ma'am," Nick swore. "Trigger is plumb tuckered out."

. . . too damned cute and fragile.

That was it. Nick was fragile at that moment. Maybe while he slept, I could find something in his room. Some proof.

Bingo!

Everyone in the house was already bedded down to recover from the previous night's rigors, so there was no secrecy necessary in our trudge to the master suite. Nick stripped down to his skivvies and burrowed under the covers, putting out one big arm of invitation. I pulled the shades, which did not have nearly as many rips in them as I expected, so that the room was somewhat darkened.

And as I did so, I checked out the position of drawers, closets, and heaps of clothing for later inspection.

I am not nearly as ditzy as my family believes.

How could I be?

Crawling under the covers, I allowed Nick to cuddle up behind me as I faced the door. Just like fire drill in school: know your exits. As soon as he loosened his grip, I could do some exploring. Within a minute, Nick's gentle snuffling was blowing into the hair at my neck. Aside from the prednisone, the doctor at the hospital had given every victim (notice how I could use the word *victim* rationally?) a healthy squirt of a tranquilizer. Nick adjusted his left arm under mine and pulled me closer, his breathing becoming slower and deeper.

I counted.

And counted.

And slept right up until Jonathan pounded on the door to get me up to heat up the soup for the cast.

Jonathan followed me to the kitchen. His size had, apparently, made him more impervious to poison and drugs than the slightest members of the cast.

"You are such a slut," he said, handing me a (thanks, Sis) clean pot from a cabinet.

"You better watch what you say to the person preparing your food, there, buddy," I advised and started looking for a can opener. There was an electric one, but it was, naturally, not working. At the opposite side of the kitchen I spotted another, which *was* working.

SS rule number forty-seven: broken thing may be replaced, but broken thing must remain forever in original spot.

"Oh, have a butt, you slut," Jonathan said, slipping a lit one between my lips as I dumped cans into the aluminum pressure cooker.

"Thanks, Fuhrer. You may just have saved your own life."

"Ain't that the truth." He leaned against the countertop, still a bit wobbly, but rapidly coming back to his old rabid self. "So? How is he?" he leered.

I lit the propane gas stove with a match and did a model's turn as I put the pot on to boil.

"I believe you found me dressed, did you not?"

"I did. So how was he?"

"You know what your problem is, Resnick? You," I stuck a finger into his face, "are a closet heterosexual. That's why you hate women. It's because you *want* us." I stirred the broth. Frankly, I still do not know whether broth needs to be stirred or if it can simply be left to its own devices. Anyway, it was nothing more than a prop at that moment.

"I need this show, Vic," Jonathan said, ignoring my fatuous accusation. "I'm kissing forty, and I really need this show." He meant *Oh, Mac!* naturally. Professionally, both of us needed a fifth production of anything like we needed another rectum.

"I know, Jon. We'll come through, honey. We always do." And that was the truth. The truth was also that we had never had to step around barbecued actors before, either, but I sure as hell wasn't going to say so.

"I love him, Vic." Jon took an enormous drag off his cigarette. "I wouldn't do anything to hurt Little Jon, you know that."

"I know that." I was stirring again, now so that Jonathan

could continue spilling his guts without being embarrassed by my looking at him with, egad, sympathy.

"Someone is out to close my show before it opens." I stirred on in silence. It seemed likely. "You don't think," he paused, stubbed out his cigarette and lit another, "Little Jon could hate me that much, do you?"

In fact I did. They had loved each other so much and for so long that I certainly did believe it could turn that hateful. Where had I heard *that* one before. Ah, yes, Nick.

What I did not believe, was that Little Jon had the variety of skills and knowledge to arrange the plethora of accidents plaguing the theater. Besides, he was a dancer and would never risk permanent damage to his legs from a fall from the scaffolding. He was limber, but no stunt man.

"I know Little Jon is not the one. I'm sure, Jonathan," I answered another question entirely. One of my many fortes. Wit and parry, wit and parry. I turned off the heat on the stove. "Soup's on," I announced.

"Better call the troupe," Jonathan said. "I want them up and running for early rehearsal tomorrow. "They'll keep their strength up if it kills them."

Boy, was I glad *I* didn't say that.

But I might as well have.

FOURTEEN

I DELUDED MYSELF into surprise and chagrin that one lousy bowl of broth could bring Trigger back to full health and glossy coat.

I wish I could say it was a guilty conscience that snuck me out the door in the middle of the night and back to my own room. Truthfully, it was fatigue seasoned with just a touch of fear. I fell asleep far too late into the morning with the open script to *Oh, Mac!* balanced on my stomach. Rehearsals always come too early in the day—even when they are held at night.

Healthier-looking groups have marched out of prisoner-of-war camps than that which staggered down the hill from the cast house to the theater that Tuesday morning. I think the knowledge that we would be performing *Whorehouse* again that night did nothing to energize the actors. Everyone knows that physical point where it is not possible to go on any further.

We were beyond that. Which, in optimistic actor-think, meant the worst was over. It had to be.

Jonathan did not bother with a sing-through. We would all be needing our voices for the show that evening. Even with vocal rest, we would sound like a pack of braying mules, but that was the luck of the draw. At least my smoking ban was over. It worried me that Jonathan had called it off. It meant that, somehow, he had given up. Like a man with a shot to the heart, he just kept moving forward, not realizing that he was dead on his feet. So instead of singing, Jonathan started to block the show.

Now, one of the nicest things about being a character leading lady (except for Auntie Mame, the nonmusical) is that even though the audience thinks we carry the show, we tend to be onstage less than almost anybody. Such was the case with Lady M.

So, ironically (and is there any other way?) the healthiest member of the cast was the first one released from rehearsal.

On my way out, I noticed Susan napping on a pile of papers at her desk in the office and Charlie building sets with Buck in the field behind the barn. Mr. Mike was standing around in the sun without a shirt on observing and, one hopes, learning something. Bones jutted out from beneath pimply skin. The picture of disenfranchised youth. I hoped the sun would do something to clear up his skin.

Who says I'm not a kind person deep, deep down inside?

And who says I move like a cow? I evaded the whole bunch of potential witnesses and made my way stealthily as a cat up the hill to the deserted house.

I knew it would take at least another two hours of blocking to get to the part of the play where my character descends into utter madness. A short step down off the curb, Dan would say. Nonetheless, I would have the house to myself.

As soon as I walked in the door, I called out to confirm that I was alone. At last. There was a barely readable note stuck on the pay phone telling me that Dan "Duchess" had returned my call.

Yeah, well, too little too late, buddy.

This was *my* mission. No ex-husband, no cop, no sister to get in *my* way. No siree bob. I started in the basement where two interns were lodged and worked my way up.

The cellar was dank, dirty, and low-ceilinged. Two mattresses were propped up on planking at one corner of the dungeon wanna-be opposite the furnace and water heater. A peeling, shockingly blue chest of drawers leaned menacingly away from the unfinished rock walls. On its surface lay two marijuana roaches and an art deco hash pipe.

Well, at least the apprentices came from money this year, I thought.

I also thought that if the weather got really steamy, these would be the choicest beds in the joint.

As far as I could tell, after searching the drawers, the youngsters were relatively clean livers. Not so much as an aspirin to be found. Either they had not yet discovered the propranolol trick, or they were too young to get really nervous.

On the second floor, Khaki's room was next on my agenda. As understudy, she only had to share with one other actor. The room was every bit as tidy as I expected, with new curtains hung at the windows, and cute little personal items of Khaki's neatly arranged on one nightstand directly beneath a signed 8-by-10 glossy of Barbra Streisand.

"Quelle suprise," I muttered aloud. I really must start working on my jaded attitude.

Maybe not.

Khaki's nightstand drawer yielded a panorama of pharmaceuticals—prescription and over-the-counter. I learned that Khaki was medicating for an ulcer, migraines, constipation as well as diarrhea (good Lord), hemorrhoids, irregular menstruation, indigestion, gas, water retention, and—there we go—stage fright. A prescription label clearly displayed her name and the container was half-empty. That gave me pause.

Half a bottle would not have been enough to poison the entire cast and the date of the prescription was old—filled at her last theater job somewhere in regional-theater purgatory. Shamokin Dam, Pennsylvania. I don't mind telling you, *that* made me feel guilty.

Poor Khaki was not only a hypochondriac, but she was being one in the middle of every noplace in America.

The only interesting item scrounged from Khaki's roommate's drawers was a collection of condoms that would make Bob Guccione envious. The poor young girl had not yet figured out that about the last place in the world she would need such protection would be in a musical production in the backwoods of Maine, unless she had Martha Stewart plans to crochet herself a tarp. The chance of having a spare straight man in the ensemble was about as good as encountering a local man who would want to talk to an actor, let alone bring one home to mother.

Knowledge is not always a good thing.

All the other rooms turned up a variation on the theme. Lots of prophylactics and barely touched bottles of beta-blockers. The biggest intellectual breakthrough I had was that I ought to recommend to Charlie and Susan that they install a washer and dryer somewhere in the house.

Of course, I had saved the scariest for last.

Nick's room.

First, I washed my hands. Second (yes, I was stalling), I

dropped into my own room to change into lighter clothing. The temperature outside had reached about eighty-five and I was sweating like a pig.

Nerves might have had something to do with it. I had not put on my watch and really did not know how long I had been rifling through other people's personal belongings.

Lydia was wrong again. If for no other reason than that, I would assuredly burn in hell. Which reminded me.

A quick check reassured me that the incriminating contracts I had hidden at the bottom of my suitcase under that dippy cardboard piece that is supposed to keep the luggage square, but mostly just flips around sucking up loose change and airline tickets. I needed to be sure that no one else was as unscrupulous as I.

What a relief.

Still, I sat on the side of my bed for several minutes before I could summon up the courage to snoop through Nick's privacy. Odd, isn't it, that you can be naked with another person and still be embarrassed over something as petty, crass, and vulgar . . .

Well, that line of thought was getting me nowhere fast. What does E. Jean Carroll say at the end of her show, "Ask E. Jean"? Oh, yes. "Fate *loves* the fearless!"

Remind me that I have been watching too many television talk shows.

In the hall, I called out once more, loudly. It was blatant fear, but then fate has never gone to more effort than to tolerate me—and then, only with disinterest. Mostly, it doesn't even do that.

My voice bounced off the walls innocently enough. I listened for a response and got none, save the creaking of the old pine flooring beneath my feet.

My threshold of guilt was being sorely tested. On the other hand, since I obviously was not capable of keeping myself fully clothed anywhere near Nick Jacobs, I really owed it to myself to feel safe enough after I had sinned to drift off into sleep like a normal, American slutress.

How is *that* for rationalization?

I thought so, too, as I cracked open the door. All but one of the shades was still drawn, so the light was not what I had hoped for, and some part of me couldn't go the whole nine yards to turning on a light. I don't know why.

Somehow it would have made the entire search seem so, well, premeditated.

The closet was filled with too many clothes. Experienced actors take as few belongings as they can to summer stock because we know we will never have an opportunity to wear anything nice anyway. Plus, we mere dirt-coolies also have to carry our own luggage. That, alone, is enough to make us minimalists. But, then, Nick Jacobs was no ordinary summer stock actor.

I had an involuntary shudder of desire at the scent of his Givenchy cologne, which I thought was unfairly distracting. And diverting.

With renewed determination, I stumbled over the edge of the bed getting to the nightstand.

Perspiration was running in an unattractive way down my forehead and into my eyes, but the room was not all that warm. I was going to have a bruise the size of Delaware on my shin by show time that night.

"And what else is new?" I could hear all my nearest and dearest asking in unison from somewhere inside my insecure little brain.

I *knew,* from distinctly personal experience, that I would be running across a panapoly of latex in Nick's drawer. So typical that I could be safe *and* sorry.

Wrong again. Okay, actually, not. But Nick had not packed preparing to cut a swathe through the entire female population of New England. There was only one, no-frills Trojan in the corner of the drawer. And it was a documented left-oversight.

For some reason, that made me feel even *worse*.

There was a beaten up copy of—jeez, why me?—my favorite book ever: Larry McMurtry's *Lonesome Dove*. Pile that kind of evidence up with *Robin and Marian* and good cognac, and what you get is a woman with a burgeoning desire to throw herself in front of a train for some very suspicious, probably homicidal, Y-chrome. I wanted to blame my hormones, but that would have been cheating.

I hated myself. But then, you knew that.

I hated myself worse when my fingers wrapped themselves around a large, industrial-sized prescription bottle.

And when I rattled it, heard the give-away clinking of perhaps three tablets, and read the pharmacy label, I hated my parents for contributing the genetic material that could result in progeny as numb-as-a-fart, butt-stupid as me.

Nick had filled a prescription for two hundred propranolol tablets less than one month before at an apothecary somewhere in Beverly Hills, California. And he was ready for a refill. I dropped the bottle as though it were molded from stinging nettles, and it landed directly on top of what appeared to be an urgent note from Nick's agent.

Numbly, I walked over to the unshaded window to read it: NICK—Your agent called re: S.C. Prods. Call back ASAP!

I cannot describe to you how much I wanted the initials

S.C. to mean South Carolina, but I couldn't convince myself. Not after seeing the bottle of beta-blockers. S.C. meant Sweet Cheeks. Nick must have been pressed seamless to the wall for him to be discussing his checkered past with an outside source. Agents are not quite the sweethearts they would like us to believe.

Slam!

The rusty front screen door smashed against the jamb, and a pair of very heavy feet were sprinting up the stairs.

Without thinking (altogether now: *Quelle surprise!*), I shoved the note from Nick's agent into my shoe and threw myself down on the bed.

My first prayer was that it was not Nick who had returned, and my second was that I hoped I had landed in provocative position just in case it *was* Nick who had unceremoniously come home to roost. My third prayer was really just an actor's mantra. That is, please Raja Whoha, let the light be dim enough that I look good, because I don't have a snowball's chance of getting out of this on ability or intelligence.

The footsteps stopped down the hall. My guess was, directly in front of my own door. Then I heard a light tap, tap, tapping. Because I am basically a moron, I relaxed a bit. Someone had been sent to wake me to get back to rehearsal, that was all. I could sneak back to theater as soon as it was safe and claim I was, I don't know, killing rats with a broom in the attic.

"Vic!"

Nick stood in the doorway.

I did not think it possible to gag one's own heart right up the trachea and then swallow it down again, but it is.

"Hi, honey. Tough day at the office?" I tap danced.

Yep, definitely going to burn in hell, and undoubtedly

going to get there faster than I had planned.

"Baby," Nick whispered. My aorta was thumping like a flat tire on a freeway. "I'm sorry, baby, I didn't want to wake you if you were sleeping." God, the man is smooth.

I am about to die, and there I lay thinking, Wow.

Okay, I thought. You've been married. You've had sex when nauseous, disinterested, and flat-out asleep. You can do this, Vic.

What really scared me, I think, is that the prospect really didn't bother me all that much. Jonathan was right. If that isn't slut-thinking (or lack thereof), I don't know what is.

Nick sat on the edge of the big bed and leaned over to kiss me.

"Poor baby, it must be ninety in here." He wiped the sweat from my cheek. "I'll open the windows all the way and damn the mosquitoes."

And full speed ahead.

You know, there are some days when Valium is just not enough.

"I'm fine, Nick," I said.

"Oh, don't sell yourself short," he said, walking to the windows. "Besides, I'd kind of like to be able to see you." He flipped open two windows and light poured in the room. "Hope you don't think that's kinky."

Noooooooo. Who me? Think that getting naked and doing the big dirty with a man she has just discovered is within one red hair of being a mass murderer is kinky?

Not Vic Bowering.

"We're not needed back at the theater for about fifteen minutes," he murmured into my hair, working my tennis shorts down my thighs. "So what is madame's pleasure? One medium or two quickies?" Oh, wow, could that man kiss.

Oh, wow. My ballet slipper. The note from Nick's agent in the ballet slipper.

"Two quickies, please," I answered, thinking that quickies could be logically accomplished with shoes on. Men have sex all the time wearing socks, don't they? These were pink slippers. Maybe he wouldn't even notice that I had them on.

You see? what was left of my conscience whined at me. *You see what happens when you're left on your own?*

"Let me undress you," Nick said as he pulled my McAleer's T-shirt over my head. It stuck to my skin, but still he was gentle. I was braless, to which he paid proper attention, so I took the opportunity to try to urge him onto his back for me to strip him down and possibly do what a woman's gotta do, shoes on. "Oh, no you don't. I know my job." He stopped me and pulled the shorts down my calves to my ankles. With a flourish, he whipped them off along with, naturally, my slippers. Nick held the entire mass in one hand and lowered himself over me.

Maybe everything would be all right. The slippers were very soft and squooshy and balled up very neatly into his big hand. The hand went up, cotton and leather and all, over my head as he kissed me again. My urgent kiss in response was as truly urgent as any kiss I'd ever given.

In the throes of passion, I could just shove the incriminating Capezio over the side of the bed and collect the product of my indiscretion at my leisure. Or, better yet, while Nick was showering, I could put it back where it belonged! At last, a concept!

"What's this?" Nick asked, his head angled up above mine. He scrambled over my body to sit upright. Oh, yeah, it was the note.

I swiped the T-shirt off the pillow and pulled it over my head while Nick stared at the message, literally open-mouthed.

"You have been going through my things!" he accused with just the right touch of outrage. I couldn't find my panties or shorts and silently thanked Kerry McAleer for having his promotional tees cut just a little too long for humans. "Why, Vic?"

Oh, and the hell with the shoes, too. Aborigines go barefoot all the time. No big deal. I backed away from the big man.

He stood, crushing the yellow Post-It Note in one hand. I bit my bottom lip hard enough to taste blood in my mouth.

Nick stood like a statue of Zeus between me and the door, except I was so terrified, I believe I could have knocked over a mere marble monolith. Unfortunately, the window was out of the question.

If I did not slash myself to death going through the already cracked panes, I would surely break my neck in the fall. So, I did the only rational thing.

I charged the door, totally bare-assed. He caught me as easily as a dusty moth at the end of the season and covered my mouth with the palm of his hand. The scent of Givenchy made my stomach clutch.

"Hello! Anybody home?" Susan's voice carried up the stairwell from the front door.

And just like the doomed moth of late fall, I flailed against something bigger, brighter, and hotter than I.

"You and I," Nick whispered into my ear, "have to have a *talk*. You understand?"

"Anybody?" Susan called again.

I nodded as much as I could manage, given the tightness with which Nick was holding my chin and neck.

The sound of a door closing made me think of the final

165

sealing of a coffin. It made me think of Dan and Barry, and it made me want my baby sister.

This is what you wanted, Vic, raged my obnoxious inner child. I guess autonomy isn't all that it's cracked up to be, is it? I guess Vic Bowering can't even learn anything from a war in f'ing *Bosnia,* can she? Well, you idiot, you're alone now. Really, really alone.

But isn't it said that everyone is alone?

When they die?

FIFTEEN

I HAVE ALWAYS told my sister, Lydia, that one of the main reasons we are both so warped is that our father never wanted sons.

He always found it so much more eccentric to raise daughters as though they *were* sons.

The reason my sister is so much more likeable than I—and I could admit this to myself since I was on the teetering edge of being mulch anyway—is that I took to the whole weird concept more easily than she did.

She used to sneak around being pretty and nice. She hid it from our dad, but the truth is, that is just her nature. My nature, according to Mother, is simply uncategorizable. So, people do not get as pissed off with Lydia as they do with me. I can accept it; I've been in therapy.

It was all Dad's fault.

On the other hand (and there is *always* another hand), Dad's philosophy on sex education for me was a five-minute demo on how to kill a man with one blow, which for a woman living in New York City can be very handy. How utterly impish of fate that I should have to dredge up that one father-"son" talk in the middle of some township in Maine that did not even have a Woolworth's.

Killing machine lesson number one: drive the palm of the hand into the bad guy's nose, driving the bone into the cerebrum.

Well, that was no good, since my hands were pinned.

Lesson number two: with the side of the hand or straightened knuckles (mind you, don't make a fist, or you'll hurt yourself), crush the larynx and esophagus of the nasty person.

Also no good for same reason.

Last-ditch lesson number three: the old knee-to-the-groin bit. Nonlethal, but a quick stop. Dad would have been so disappointed in me.

The knee slammed up, and thanks to all the dance training I bitched and complained through, it is a very strong knee, indeed.

Innocently, I expected him to get off me, not fall straight down as he did. But as Nick curled himself into a little ball, physics was on my side and I just rolled him off.

"Je*sus,* Vic!" Nick squeezed out from his compressed diaphragm, and I shot out of the room like compressed air through a leaky gasket.

The carpet on the stairs had not been vacuumed since God's mother was young, and I sliced open the pads of both feet within three steps. I guess that would teach me not to be an aborigine. I was learning a lot that day.

From the first-landing window I spotted Susan's car still parked at the back of the cast house. I would be safe if only I could catch her before she drove off. I could already hear Nick coming down the hall toward the stairs and after me. Need I say, he did not sound in a playful mood? Need I say, that of all the people who might be chasing me to do me abject bodily harm, I would pick the one person with a longer stride than mine? I could never make it to the theater before he caught me.

Fortunately, Nick was hobbling a little.

I swung myself off the newel post at the end of the stairs and propelled myself out the door and around the corner of the house to Susan's car. The keys dangled forlornly off the souvenir Vacationland lobster key-ring. That could only mean that Susan was still in the house.

And if Susan were still in the house, that meant that the door Nick and I heard must be the only other one in the building that has slamming capability. And that door was in the kitchen. I saw one of Nick's feet lower itself carefully onto one of the higher stair treads and raced into the kitchen.

I would like to tell you I had a plan, but I didn't, beyond finding someone to at least witness my ignominious end. Yet, when I spotted the basement door, I remembered moldering piles of old tools that were better than nothing in the mutual arms race. Susan must have gone down there, because she sure wasn't on the first floor.

I was huffing enough air from my belabored lungs to blow-dry an entire cast of *Steel Magnolias*. Screaming, though, seemed to be entirely beyond my respiratory capabilities. Just my luck.

As quietly as I could, I closed the cellar door and felt my way down the splintery stairs in the darkness. Even if for no reason I could think of, Susan had left her car and keys at the cast house, I believed I remembered a crumbling bulkhead through which I could flee, if necessary.

Just like fire drill. Know your exits. I just wished there had been enough light down there to *see* an exit. My sense of direction is not, honestly, all that it could be.

Over the moldy, dank basement smell, I could make out a heavier musk. The further into the bowel of the cellar, the stronger it got and I was not exactly speeding along.

Breaking a leg would not be to my advantage at that stage of the game, so I carefully felt my way along the low-hung rafters that served as a ceiling. All the while my nerves were pumping. Talk about stage fright. Cobwebs replete with husks of small insects and the fat bodies of active spiders caught between my fingers and under my nails. I would have paid a week's wages—with rehearsal stipend—to have been able to shout "Yechhhhh," but fate does not make those kinds of bargains and I kept my big, fat, stupid mouth shut.

Overhead I could hear Nick stumbling around.

"Vic," he called. "Vic, what the hell is happening here?"

"Shhhh."

My outflung hands rested on the chest of another person in that damnable black hole, and the chest had boobs.

"Susan?" I whispered. The "other smell" had begun to override the pervasive basement odor. It was natural gas. Quite a bit of it.

"Yes, Vic, it's me. I'm here. You're all right now."

"Susan, oh, God, Susan. It was Nick. We have to get out of here. Do you have a light?"

"Yes, Vic, I do, but it wouldn't be a good idea to turn it on. There's a gas leak and any spark could cause an explosion."

"Right," I agreed, nodding in the blackness. "Right."

My eyes were beginning to adjust to the tiniest glimmer of daylight forcing its way through the grimy slot window next to the phantom bulkhead. There were structural cracks in the wooden double doors, which led me to believe that even in our weakened states, Susan and I could break through to fresh air and freedom.

You see, I had already forgotten that precious bit of wisdom that flashed through my mind when I was certain Nick Jacobs was going to snuff out that shining stardom I like to believe is hiding somewhere inside me.

It is said that everyone is alone.

Just my luck that when I am not, I am with a woman who is about to club me to death with a tetanus-laden two-by-four, nail-studded for full effect.

To be fair, she was a woman with very good manners.

"I'm sorry, Vic," Susan said.

"Susan, did you turn the gas on purposely?"

Talk, just keep talking. Women are communicators. I had heard that on *Geraldo* just the day before I left to come to the best little slaughterhouse in Maine.

"I had to. I didn't want to, but I really had to. Nothing else worked, you see."

"I do. I do, Susan, you had to. I mean, it makes sense. Rehearsal will be over in about an hour, and you knew that Jonathan or I would light a cigarette the minute we got in the door."

"Oh, Vic, no. I was hoping one of you would walk in with a lit cigarette. I don't want more people to die than absolutely have to."

"I know that, Susan."

This communication thing seemed to be working, but the smell of gas was getting to be a bit much. If one is unconscious, verbal skills decline considerably.

I guess Susan was on the same wavelength, because at that moment I could see the shadow of her arm rise. Immediately, I stepped back.

Into a support beam. A nail or hook snagged my T-shirt and through to the skin, ripping both as I clumsily threw myself to the side—and into a workbench. My feet were tangled in old clothing, ropes, and cast-off lumber, and I was literally hanging from a post as Susan repositioned herself and took a deep breath.

I was blinded by the flash of nightmarish light. My ears rang with the clattering thump and my feet were pinned in position.

But they were hurting like hell, which, under the circumstances, seemed like a good thing.

"Get out, Vic," Nick shouted at me from within inches. "I'll carry Susan."

"I don't . . ."

"Get out! Follow the light!"

How droll. As far as I could figure, I had been blown into cat food, and was now trapped forever in a rerun of *Poltergeist*.

Nick grabbed my arm and led me out the shattered bulkhead door. He dumped the unconscious form of Susan in the overgrown weeds beside me and lunged back into the basement.

As for myself, I threw up. I guess it was my turn.

"You okay, Vic?" Nick asked me when I had at last finished purging myself.

"If I'm not dead, I'd say I'm just fine, thank you." Then I remembered our little misunderstanding. "How are you?"

"Adjusting to the idea of never fathering a child, thank you."

"Nick, I'm sorry."

"Write it down. I want to remember those words always." He was still angry. I can tell these things. Susan moaned deeply from the grass. From down the hill I could hear voices, telling me that rehearsal was over and the cast would be at the house in five minutes or so. Susan's weeping broke through spates of coughing.

"Oh, Susan," I sighed. "Why? I don't understand."

"Vic, you are such a child." She snuffled and went on. "You can't be more than ten years younger than me and you're still a baby. Why, you ask? Why?

"Because I can't take my show on the road any more. Charlie and I have spent decades building, losing, rebuilding, dreaming, and redreaming. It had to stop. Charlie was killing himself and me. His heart, you know. At best, I won't have my husband for more than another few years and I wanted him. I deserved my husband.

"I couldn't get Charlie to leave this life, so I had to find a way to get the life to leave us. To leave us *alone.*"

"Mike!" Nick shouted. "Go back to the theater and bring back Verenes."

"But, Nick," Mike whined, "it's only an hour before I have to be back at the theater and I . . ."

"Do it!"

I held Susan in my arms and made up cooing noises that sounded to me as though they might be comforting. I couldn't be sure, but I thought Lydia would be proud of me.

Charlie and Chief Verenes were at our sides almost before I had hit a comfort-rhythm. My rocking technique was smoothing out, too.

I would like you to believe I was doing it for Susan's sake, but it was as much for me as it was for her. The moment she was taken away and the crowd of actors had cleared, I didn't know what to do with myself.

Nick had lain back into the grass to watch the sunset. After everything I had done to him it seemed rude to just walk away. He might have preferred it. I'll probably never know.

"I was so wrong, Nick."

"That's what my first wife said."

"No. I mean it."

"Second wife." He continued to watch the birds start settling in for the evening song and waited. "Why don't you just talk to me the way the woman I hope to meet someday would?"

"Because it's too hard?"

"Third wife."

I lay back in the antsy weeds next to my leading man.

"Okay, think you can take it, big guy?"

Together we said, "Fourth wife," and I continued alone. "Garrett had contracts hidden in her room for a porn flick you two made back in the early eighties. Okay, who cares besides your mother."

"And my public," he added sourly.

"Right. I thought Garrett might have been blackmailing you. It does make some sense, doesn't it?" He nodded nobly. "And I didn't believe you were lovers—I'd never read that you were, and the way you were with me—well, damn it. Damn, damn. Blackmail seemed the only thing that fit."

"So you thought I fried her like so many chitlins?" Nick's photographic green eyes glistened in the twilight. I nodded, so ashamed I thought I would never get over it. Actually, I still haven't.

"No," I protested. Nick shook his head slowly, silently asking me not to lie.

"That picture was never released, Vic. I know you'll find it hard to believe, but Garrett and I weren't very good actors then.

The original tapes were destroyed along with all other 'assets' in the insurance fire in eighty-three."

"But the propranolol . . ."

". . . you found while tossing my room. I confess. I get stage fright. I was taking so many of those suckers before every show, I have the resistance of a horse. I could have eaten four of those spiked lunches without throwing them up." He barked what I believe was a harsh laugh. "First time I've ever been blamed for staying healthy. The producers of *Jake Manley* had an insurance policy on me to insure them against goddamn *lateness*.

"Vic, I've never been a stage actor and I guess I never will be. I don't know why I am so frigging miserable. The PR from this mess ought to kick me into feature films without so much as a sonic boom."

I knew I was just taking one last stab at redeeming myself, when it was already too late, but there was one more thing.

"Why did you insist on bringing Garrett with you here, if she wasn't blackmailing you and you weren't lovers?"

Nick gave me the answer I least wanted to hear. The sort of answer that drives a stake of shame and sorrow directly through the heart.

"She was my friend." He looked directly into my eyes. "She needed the weeks for unemployment."

"Harumphhh." Mr. Mike cleared his throat from the corner of the house. "Uh, show's canceled, guys."

"Thank you," Nick and I automatically answered together.

Boy, I had really blown this one. Sky high.

"Uh, I mean, like, forever."

"Thank you," we echoed. It really was a beautiful sunset. I wished I could pocket it and take it out whenever I needed it in the future.

"They've taken Mrs. Mackin off to Augusta State Hospital. Mr. Mackin went with her. He said for me to drive you all back to the airport or bus station whenever you . . ."

I sat up, though it was not what I had in mind. What I would have liked was to be able to go back and try not to do the same stupid, redundant things that screw up my life every time I try to *have* one.

"Ah-hmmmm," Mr. Mike tried again.

"Thank you, Mr. Mike, you have truly been a brick, and on behalf of the entire company I would like to personally extend our gratitude. Now, may we continue to watch the sky, please, in private?"

"Sure," he said with a look in his eye that clearly asked "why?"

"Ever slept in the weeds, Dale?" Nick asked.

"As a matter of fact, Roy, yes. Of course that was back in the sixties."

"Ever said good-bye lying down?"

I thought about that one for a minute. Perhaps, two. Might as well be honest; it was far too late for anything else.

"Only when I didn't know it was a real good-bye."

Nick seemed to understand that.

"Ever make love in a field before the sun went down with a house full of people probably hanging out the windows watching?"

Forgiven again, but only for what I cannot help. Not what might have been, but, hey, what is?

"Two quickies or a medium?" I negotiated.

"Long. Very long."

★ ★ ★

And so it goes. I have now done just about everything that can be done in a field, including sleeping until the birds make such a racket at the intrusion that they fly down to look you in the face.

At sunrise, Nick helped me to my feet and kissed me.

"Good-bye, Vic."

"Good-bye, Nick."

He held my face in both his hands and looked at me for some time. My hands rested on his flat belly, feeling the motions of his lungs, inhaling, exhaling. Saying good-bye without saying it.

"We loved each other, you know."

I nodded.

"Weird."

I nodded again and spoke when I could.

"Very."

Nick went back into the house and was back out with his bags and Mr. Mike within fifteen minutes. I waved from several hundred yards out in the pasture, a huge bunch of black-eyed Susans already wilting in my hand.

Still, I put the bouquet in an old mayonnaise jar and left them in the community living room before I went upstairs to pack.

I had a little trouble squeezing in the *Robin and Marian* video Nick had left on my bed, but, as always, with a little effort, it worked out in the end. Everything just came out a little wrinkled and the worse for wear.

And something new had been added.

EPILOGUE

McAleer's was waiting for me like a faithful dog after all the preliminary reentry to New York details had been taken care of.

Dan turned over my apartment keys and told me to get a good night's sleep, absolving me from the affair I could tell he knew I'd had. I resolved to make it up to him. Maybe it was time to get on with the formal divorce.

Slasher awoke from a nap looking just confused enough that I wasn't sure if he knew I had ever been away.

I stopped by Jewel LaFleur's apartment and got ripped to the tits with her on great champagne, told her everything, let her hold me like a baby and croon "Woozy, woozy woozy," and felt a little better.

I called my sister, who told me to grow up and get out of show business. And Barry, who told me the same thing and that we would discuss formalizing the dissolution of our marriage over dinner the next week.

Since it would be longer than I could afford before the

financial mess at the theater was cleared up—maybe months—and I was still short work weeks for an unemployment claim, I did the logical thing.

I waited for Timmy to come on duty at my local bar, and then went for a visit.

Shannon, one of the bartenders at Mac's, whom friends like to refer to as my evil twin since—so hard to believe—we both are the same height, size, weight, and have the same out-of-control red hair, was in conference with Kerry McAleer at the end of the bar. I was in a space-giving mood anyway.

To everyone's surprise, Shannon and I get along pretty well, as I concede she is actually better than I because of her British accent. She is most fond of being conceded to.

"You look like shit," Timmy commented as he put a Guinness and a shot of something brown in front of me.

"I missed you, too," and threw the shot directly to my aching gut. Jägermeister. Blechhh. I pushed the glass forward for another.

"Have you been gone, sweetie?" Shannon asked, blowing air kisses to both sides of my head.

"In so many ways, Shannon. How are you?"

"I am a *rag*."

Kerry came up behind both of us and ruffled our hair in unison. Shannon and I hate that.

"Buy the girls a drink, will you, Tim?"

"Buy us two, Timmy," Shannon said, all the while smiling at the owner.

"You been away?" Kerry asked me. "You look like shit."

"Okay, one last time." I tossed the shot down and took a deep breath. "Yes, I was away. I was doing summer stock with Nick Jacobs and the theater folded before I got enough weeks for unemployment, so I am sitting here at my favorite bar getting kazoshed so I can stop thinking about it before the mailman brings me another batch of bills I cannot pay."

"Oh," said Kerry, eyes brightening. "No wonder you look like shit. Want a job?"

"I beg your pardon?"

Shannon shot Kerry the sort of look that fells small woodland creatures. He amended his question.

"Know how to bartend?"

"No," I answered, half-lying. I had bartended in New England sometime during the Jurassic period. Rum and coke. Rum and coke. Beer. Beer. Beer and a shot. Whiskey sour for the lady. You know.

"So, start her on afternoons, Shannon."

"What? You just heard her say she doesn't know a gin fizz from a Frisbee." Shannon was not taking this well.

"So teach her. We're not talkin' nuclear physics here."

"When can I start?" I asked.

"Tomorrow," Kerry patted my ass as he headed for the exit. "Shannon, fire Brian first thing, okay?" And he left.

"Don't do it," Shannon warned me. "It's better to starve. Trust me."

"I should have taken you to Maine with me."

"Of course you should have, but you are forgiven. Victoria, darling—margarita, Tim, with salt—believe me, you would rather have food poisoning than this job."

"Oh, Shannon. How bad can it be?"

Shannon looked at me as though I had just been hatched.

"All right. We open at six A.M. Be here. Give Brian all the drinks he wants, and then eighty-six him. Lesson number one in how bad it can get."

Timmy poured another shot into my glass and one for himself.

"You're doomed, me darlin'. Welcome to the wonderful world of bartending."

"Everything's going to be *fine*," I toasted my new compatriots. "Just *fine*."

Oh, don't even say it.

You know how I get.